• MAURICE

# Baring

*The Lonely Lady of Dulwich*

HOUSE OF
STRATUS

This edition published in 2003 by House of Stratus, an imprint of Stratus Books Ltd., Lisandra House, Fore St., Looe, Cornwall PL13 1AD, UK.

www.houseofstratus.com

Typeset by House of Stratus.

A catalogue record for this book is available from the British Library and the Library of Congress.

ISBN 0-7551-0101-4

To
B and C

*Post tempestatem magna serenitas.*

THOMAS À KEMPIS.

# CHAPTER I

In the summer of 1919 I spent a fortnight at Haréville taking the waters. There I met an old lady whom I will call Mrs Legge. I was living at Dulwich at the time.

Mrs Legge hearing this, asked me if I had met a Mrs Harmer who lived there. I had not. In the course of the fortnight I spent at Haréville, Mrs Legge told me Mrs Harmer's story; this is the story, or rather what I have made of it.

Oliver Mostyn, half Irish, with a dash of French blood, educated in Germany and Paris and widely travelled, had been an adventurer in the best sense of the word. He had been adventurous, and adventures had come to him. In some ways he had been like Dryden's famous portrait of Buckingham: everything by starts and nothing long, nearly successful in so many enterprises and undertakings but never quite: he made a discovery just too late, someone had just made it; he had nearly won the Grand National, riding the horse that had come in fourth; he had three times almost been elected to parliament; he had once practically made a fortune, but had lost it immediately. He wrote a play which was produced and was almost a success, but the same play was soon after written by someone else, and was a success. He was a handsome, gay, popular man, good-humoured, friendly and easy. The one thing in his life which was not a failure was his marriage. His wife was an American from the South, who had been brought up in a French convent: Dolores Foyle. He had met her in Paris. This all happened a long time ago, and he was married before the days of the Second Empire. In her youth she was beautiful: transparent, fair, blue-eyed, and ethereal; the dazzle of her looks and her complexion passed quickly; but the radiance of her good humour and of an inexhaustible vein of fun remained. She had three daughters, and her whole life was spent in an arduous and, in the end, successful effort to make both ends meet. That they did meet, in spite of her husband's irrepressible and spontaneous extravagance, was due to her unobtrusive cleverness as a manager and to her unostentatious talent for housekeeping. She had been poor in her youth; she had done the housework and the cooking herself, and nobody could make a more appetising salad ora lighter omelette. Her daughters grew up extremely good-looking; and she hoped they might marry well. She took them out in London, where her husband would take a house for the season. He had to live in London sometimes – he explained – because of the racing; he was obliged to race, not for pleasure, of course; he didn't care for racing, he would say, "unless you go for the day with a pal, and even then it's a damned bore"; but he had to race from economy so as to meet his expenses. His wife never contradicted him when he said this, but merely hoped he would not lose quite as much money as at the last meeting. On the whole, he was lucky, and didn't lose much; but he certainly made nothing; for what he did win on the racecourse he lost at the clubs, playing cards.

Dolores pinned her hopes on her daughters.

The eldest was rather too like a waxwork for real beauty, and exaggerated like a child's picture of a beauty; she was born in the wrong age, and would have been perfect for the screen; nevertheless, she attracted everybody's attention and arrested the devotion of an English nobleman, Lord St Alwyn, and all seemed well. He was wealthy and of good lineage, had

2

possessed estates and a London house. Unfortunately, soon after the marriage he lost all his fortune on the Turf. Everything had to be sold; things went badly in every way; discord at home was the first result, and finally separation. His wife, Teresa, went abroad and settled in a pension at Florence; there was no divorce, as the Mostyns were Catholics. There were no children. Teresa was given an allowance by her husband's trustees, and he lived on cheerfully in debt, as before, and in grave sin with a respectable-looking widow. Everyone said he had behaved badly.

The second daughter, Agnes, a dark Juno-like figure, married a respectable but obscure Italian diplomat: one of those diplomats who seem to be sent only to the uninteresting places. She was, however, quite happy, whether at Berne, or Rio, or Cettinje.

Then there was the third daughter, Zita. Her mother, who had been in her youth better-looking than all her three daughters put together, said with a sigh that Zita was not going to be so good-looking as her sisters. She would not, in fact, hold a candle to them.

But Oliver Mostyn, who was a great connoisseur of female beauty, said that Zita would be first, and the rest nowhere, and that she would marry a millionaire. When Zita was eighteen, and just about to come out, after having spent five years at a convent, she was, in spite of her mother's dismal prognostications, a lovely creature. There was a softness and a radiance about her that made you at once think of the dawn and doves, of apple blossom and lilac and lilies of the valley.

But just as she was ready to be taken out in London, Oliver Mostyn died of a cold caught at a race meeting, much to the regret of a number of friends, especially those who played whist with him at his club, where he managed to lose everything except his temper.

Oliver's death altered the whole situation. He had left little; there was little to leave. Dolores sold what she could and migrated to the South of France, taking a cheap little apartment at Cannes, whence, after a short time, she migrated to a cheaper pension at San Remo. The first year, being in deep mourning, they spent in comparative seclusion. The next year Dolores did the best she could for Zita, who was greatly admired, but in spite of her beauty – perhaps because of it – had no success. It seemed, in fact, to keep people aloof and at a distance, until Robert Harmer appeared on the scene. It was Eastertime, and Dolores and Zita were at Nice; it was the last gay winter season of the Second Empire.

Robert Harmer was in business, a north country Englishman, a banker, successful and well-to-do. He fell in love with Zita at first sight, and determined to marry her. Before the end of a fortnight he had spoken to Dolores and had proposed to Zita. Dolores was, of course, enchanted. Did he mind Zita being a pauper? Not a bit. Did he mind the difference of religion? Not at all; not even if the children – ? No, for in those days the sons of mixed marriages could still be brought up in the religion of their father, the daughters in their mother's. Robert Harmer had no objection; he thought it did not matter what the religion of women was, and not very much what that of men might be, unless it made things inconvenient.

Zita was not in the least in love with him. So far there had been only a fleeting shadow of a romance in her life. She had been attracted by a good-looking but unsatisfactory young man who was said to be undesirable, reckless, unscrupulous, and a spendthrift. He acted on the theory that every woman is at heart a rake, and that, if you make it quite clear at once that you are yourself a rake, heart, body and soul, you are certain to find favour. The more aloof, difficult and remote a woman might seem to be, the more ardent and persistent were the advances that he made. He was generally successful. People seemed shy of Zita, and said they could not get on with her. Not so Rupert Westrel, for such was his name; he treated Zita with familiarity and ease; disguising nothing, and paying her the most outrageous compliments. Dolores was a little bit uneasy, but Rupert attracted her, and she could never resist a sense of humour, which he had in an eminent degree. He proposed to Zita, and she accepted him at once; but, as neither of them had a penny, they agreed to wait. While they were waiting, Rupert made the acquaintance of a luscious and lively American heiress. Soon, with an air of resigned martyrdom, he broke off his engagement with Zita, deeply against his will, as he explained, and shortly afterwards he was engaged to the heiress and married her. They both, it may be said, lived to regret it. Zita was not heartbroken, but she was disappointed. Rupert had been charming to her, and nobody else spoke to her at all.

Zita refused Robert Harmer's first proposal, but six months later he renewed it.

This time she consented, much to the delight of her mother. In accepting Robert, Zita had simply followed the dictates of common sense. "If I fall in love with anyone, he is sure to be undesirable, impossible, in fact," she reasoned, "because those are the people one falls in love with; and if I don't marry it means hanging round my mother's neck like a millstone, while she drags me round from pension to pension and denies herself everything. She has done that all her life. She had hopes of her other daughters; they disappointed her, and now I have the chance of making all right by marrying a man who may not be a Romeo or a Prince Charming, but is desirable, honest, kind, and well off."

Marriage was a shock to Zita, a much greater shock than she had expected. She not only discovered when she had married someone that she had married someone else, but all the facts of marriage, major and minor, were a shock and a surprise to her. They lived in the country, in a house called Wallington. Robert was as kind as possible, and wanted her to have her way in everything. There was no mother-in-law; such relations as he had were either dead or at a distance. She had nothing to complain of. He made no difficulty about her religion, and she was driven to Mass every Sunday. Zita was not particularly religious, but fulfilled her duties as a matter of course. But it was chiefly the want of any interchange of ideas or interests that surprised her. She knew less about her husband and his doings than if he had been living at the South Pole. Every Monday morning, except at Christmas, Easter, Whitsuntide and in August, he went up to London and stayed there till Friday evening, sleeping at his club, where he had a permanent bedroom. He never mentioned his affairs. He was never cross or ill-tempered. He was anxious that Zita should enjoy herself and have everything she liked. He would beg her to invite her friends to the house. She had none. Her sisters were both abroad, so was her mother; and she did not wish for the searchlight of Mrs Mostyn's all-seeing glance to be thrown on the situation.

She saw quite a number of people; there were neighbours. Robert often asked them to luncheon on Sundays, and for visits during the shooting season, in the autumn, or at Christmas. Five miles off there were Lord and Lady St Eustace, who lived childless in their historic house, where Queen Elizabeth had slept and Charles II had hidden, which was, nevertheless, often full of people, young and old, and where luncheon was laid for fourteen every day, whether there were guests or not. Then a little nearer there were Colonel Gallop and his wife, Lady Emily. He was a great deal younger than she was; they had sons and daughters. Emily Gallop was full of energy, and flattered herself she knew about almost everything on earth – the sports of men, the traditions of the army and the navy, as well as the feminine accomplishments of women; the arts as well as the crafts. She would inspect Zita's needlework and criticize it, and make her play duets with her on the pianoforte or accompany her while she herself sang. She had a robust contralto voice, and sang a little out of tune when tired; at other times she would insist on inspecting the bedrooms and the stables at Wallington, or spend an evening going through Zita's household books with her, seeing what might be reduced with advantage. She would come with her husband, whose high spirits were almost excessive, and one felt that in spite of all her energy, Emily Gallop was a little fatigued by her husband's youth. Sometimes Robert and Zita would go and stay with the Gallops. Visits in those days seldom lasted less than a week, and sometimes ten days, and even when Robert was too busy to go himself, Zita used to go by herself to long shooting parties, or in the summer to cricket weeks.

But on the whole, she did not mind these visits, for both the Gallops and the St Eustaces were friendly. Then there were many other neighbours who did not entertain, but who came for the day or for a meal: the Anglican Bishop of Easthampton, a cultivated, charming, and paradoxical divine, suspected of having leanings towards the Greek Church; and his wife, who was a mass of erudition and militant philanthropy. They never appeared on Sundays; they were too busy, but they sometimes came to dine. Then there was the local parson who lived in the village, rubicund and old-fashioned, fond of partridge-shooting and port; and his nextdoor neighbour, Charles Baxter, who was in the city, in Baxter and Coles' firm, and a great friend of Robert's. He was a bachelor, and used to come to Easthampton at Easter and Christmas, and sometimes for a week or two in September and October. He was middle-aged, but he liked the young. He was fond of racing, coursing, and Homer and Horace. His first two hobbies he was able to share with Robert Harmer; not the third; indeed, the only books at Wallington were a whole series of bound volumes of Ruff's *Guide to the Turf*; and the only instrument of culture, and indeed the only outstanding ornament in the encircling leather and rep, was a barrel-organ that imitated an orchestra and made a deafening noise.

In the autumn of the first year of her marriage Zita gave birth to a little girl, but, after a long confinement, during which her sufferings were great, the baby was stillborn. The doctors said

Zita could never have another baby. Robert took the news calmly, as if he had always expected it. Another year passed in the way which has been described. Zita never went to London; neither her mother nor her sisters came to see her. Mrs Mostyn had settled down to live with her eldest daughter, Teresa, at Florence. Business then made it necessary for Robert to go to Buenos Aires; Zita went with him. She enjoyed the journey and the new sights and sounds, and the colour; but life was not different. The only people they saw were business friends of Robert, who smoked large cigars, and occasionally the British Minister or one of the secretaries from the Legation. Zita made no friends, and the climate did not agree with her. They lived there two years.

And then one day Robert told her suddenly they were going to Paris for good, at least for some years.

They settled in Paris. Robert Harmer took the apartment and engaged the servants. He did all that. It was taken for granted Zita was incapable of any practical action. Zita thought that a new life was about to begin for her. She had not enjoyed living in the country in England; she had liked South America still less. Altogether marriage had been a shattering disillusion to her, little as she had expected. Now she was looking forward to Paris. She had never lived there, but she had been through it and heard a great deal about it from her father.

"I expect we shall get to know a lot of French people," she said to Robert the day they arrived there.

"French people keep to themselves," said Robert.

"My father used to say he knew a lot of people," she said, "such interesting people – writers."

"I don't care for Bohemians," he said, "frowsty sort of sportsmen."

"But he knew all sorts of people – doctors, lawyers, and soldiers."

"They would be too clever for me," said Robert.

"But Papa used to go racing a great deal."

"Yes, he did," said Robert, rather grimly.
After this conversation, Zita suspected the worst.

# CHAPTER II

Zita's fears were realized. Their life in Paris was just the same as it had been in England and in Buenos Aires. Robert invited either his partner or a business friend to luncheon or to dinner; they talked business and smoked large cigars. Robert went to the races when he could. They knew no French people; they left cards at the Embassy, and went to one garden-party at the end of the summer. The theatres were shut. Once or twice they dined at a *café chantant* out of doors. Robert took Zita to the Opera once, but slept through the performance. Zita spent much time by herself. She drove in the Bois in the afternoon, and sometimes went to picture galleries with her maid.

Zita had only one friend, Flora Sutton, the wife of a stockbroker, a friend of Robert's, who often came over for the races, or just for pleasure. Robert had let Wallington for five years, and in August he took a shooting-lodge in the north of Scotland and invited three men friends beside Wilfred Sutton and his wife.

To the outward world Zita appeared to be neither happy nor unhappy; she had for the moment lost the radiance she had had as a girl – it had been drenched and saturated in tears – but this was not surprising, after her sojourn in the trying climate of South America. People said the elements of beauty were still there undiminished, though temporarily eclipsed. She and her husband had arrived in Paris at the end of one summer; a year passed and then another, when they again went to Scotland and entertained the same guests, and things might have gone on for ever had it not been for the advent of a new Second Secretary at the British Embassy. His name was Cyril Legge. He was forty-two years old: he had been already to Paris, Berlin, Buenos Aires, Rome and Constantinople. He had a literary vein and was slightly Bohemian, but he was thought to be a good man of affairs, in spite of that, and a successful diplomat. He was popular; foreigners liked him. When he was thirty and *en poste* at Rome he had met Amelia Foster, Robert Harmer's first cousin, and married her; they had two children. They were poor, but Amelia was clever and practical, and Cyril was a good manager, too; they were devoted to each other and got no end of fun out of life.

Cyril arrived at Paris late in July to take up his duties. It was his first morning at the Chancery, and he was sitting in the little room which was his by right, he being head of the Chancery, when the Chancery servant brought him a card bearing on it the name of Robert Harmer. The name conveyed nothing to Legge, but the Chancery servant explained that the visitor said he was a cousin of Madame's.

"I suppose I must see him," Legge said, with a sigh. "Show him in."

In walked a tall and large middle-aged man with an open-air complexion and shrewd eyes. Legge greeted him as if he had been awaiting his arrival with impatience.

"I am Amelia's first cousin," said the visitor. "I only heard yesterday that you had arrived."

"Of course," said Legge, who had no idea which cousin he might be, and knew nothing about him. "Amelia hasn't arrived yet. I'm alone. We've taken a flat, a little apartment, but we can't get into it until the end of the month, so Amelia has taken the opportunity to stay with her mother. The Ambassador is very kindly putting me up till she comes. She won't be here for another month."

There was a pause.

Harmer evidently had some subject on his mind which he found some difficulty in broaching.

"I think you know Sutton," he said, "he's on the Stock Exchange. He's been staying here; he came over for the Grand Prix."

Cyril recollected a prosperous, cultivated and rather sleek young man whom he had sometimes seen at the St James's Club.

"Well, he knows all about pictures and furniture and all that… and he was saying that Zita…that my wife ought to be painted. The question is, who is to do it? It would have to be done here, you see, because I spend any holidays I get shooting in Scotland. He advised me to consult you, and when he mentioned your name, knowing, of course, you were Amelia's husband, I thought you wouldn't mind."

"Of course I'd do anything to help," said Legge. "Sutton would know far more about it than I do. I haven't been here long, and it's ten years since I was here *en poste*. That was before the war."

"If we were in England," said Harmer, "it would be easy to get a fellow who's in the Academy; but who could do it here?"

Harmer talked as if they were on a desert island.

"I think there are still plenty of painters," said Legge, inwardly amused. "What did Sutton think?"

"He told me of a fellow called Bertrand."

"Ah," said Legge.

He knew Bertrand's work; he wondered what Mrs Harmer was like, and whether she was to have a voice in the matter; so far it did not seem as if she were.

"You've never met my wife," said Harmer, "but I think you know her sister, Lady St Alwyn."

"Oh yes, we met at Rome; she was very kind to us."

Legge now understood who Mrs Harmer was. He was at

once interested.

"I believe Bertrand is thought to be one of the coming men," he said. "He hasn't quite arrived yet, but I think he will, and that has the advantage of making him less expensive," he said, with a twinkle.

"It's not so much the money I mind," said Harmer, "but I want, you know, the kind of picture one can hang on one's walls at home without having to explain to everyone who and *what* it is."

"I think his pictures are thought like," said Legge.

"Is he in Paris now?"

"We can easily find out."

Legge soon discovered where he lived. Harmer still looked helpless. Legge thought he saw the difficulty.

"I know a friend of Bertrand's," he said, "would you like me to get him to get Bertrand to make an appointment with us, and we could go together to his studio? We should see some of his work there, and if you liked it you could arrange for sittings."

Harmer said that would suit him exactly. Legge supposed that Mrs Harmer would accompany them, or, at any rate, be consulted.

"Then I will let you know what he says," was all he said.

"Thanks most awfully," said Harmer. "As soon as Amelia arrives you must let me know, and come and have a meal in my house. I want her to know – my wife."

Harmer went away. Legge arranged the meeting with Bertrand through an old French friend of his, a connoisseur of pictures and a friend of artists, and a few days later he was able to write to Harmer telling him of the date and hour of an afternoon appointment suggested by Bertrand.

Harmer wrote that he would call for Legge in his carriage half an hour before the time mentioned. Legge was curious to see, when the time for the appointment came, whether Harmer would bring his wife with him or not. He arrived at the appointed time by himself. They drove to the studio, which was on the other side of the river.

Bertrand received them. He at once made a favourable impression on Harmer; firstly, because he was dressed neither in a blouse nor in black velvet, but just like anyone else; his hair was of the ordinary length. Secondly, he spoke English. He had lived in England at various periods of his life. Thirdly, he was utterly unaffected.

On an easel there was the portrait of an English lady, the wife of a well-known statesman. She was painted in an evening gown of pale yellow satin. Legge recognised the original of the picture at once.

"Mrs H.," he said, "I think it's wonderfully good."

Bertrand did the honours of his studio and offered Harmer a glass of Madeira and some cakes. Harmer sipped the Madeira, which he hated doing between meals. He said he thought the studio must be convenient, that he knew nothing about art himself, but that he liked a portrait to be like: that of Mrs H. was a speaking likeness. Bertrand showed them a few landscapes he had done, and apologized for showing landscapes to an Englishman, as "the English are the masters of us all," he said, "in landscape."

Harmer was surprised at finding that Bertrand was so young – he was not more than thirty-five – and he had an idea that all successful painters were at least fifty years old. They talked about England: Cambridge, where Bertrand had lived for a term; the Norfolk Broads, Scotland, the Yorkshire Moors, English gardens, and the Thames, and then suddenly Harmer looked at his watch and said he must he going, and as they went to the door he mumbled to Bertrand:

"I wonder, Monsieur Bertrand, whether you would paint me a portrait of my wife?"

Bertrand said he would be charmed. "But perhaps," he said, "Madame Harmer would not care for my style of painting."

"Oh yes, she would," said Harmer.

"When could she come and sit?"

"She can come any time, and you must make the picture any size you like."

A date was fixed. Nothing was said about the price. That matter had already been dealt with through the good offices of Legge and his friend, the connoisseur, and Harmer was perfectly satisfied with the sum that had been mentioned.

But Legge wondered more than ever what Mrs Harmer's attitude was, and would be, and he wrote that night a long letter to his wife, whom he justly considered the most sensible person in the world. He wrote describing Harmer's visit in detail.

# CHAPTER III

When Harmer told Zita that he had arranged for her to sit to Bertrand for her portrait, she was less surprised than she might have been, because Wilfred Sutton had reported to his wife what Harmer had told him, and Flora Sutton had told Zita. She had seen a picture by Bertrand at an exhibition, and had liked it; but she told Flora Sutton she was quite indifferent who should paint her, and was only pleased with anything that satisfied Robert. Robert took his wife to the studio on his way to his office, and left her there. He would send his carriage to fetch her.

Bertrand was astounded when he saw her; Legge had told him that she was supposed to be good-looking, and that she was one of three beautiful sisters; but he expected something large, British, a full-blown Romney, or else a haggard Pre-Raphaelite – too tall and too thin. But Zita was neither.

She was beautiful, in spite of looking listless and pale at the moment. Yes, she was beautiful, more than beautiful, he thought, and he wondered why she was so particularly beautiful; and he wondered for the millionth time at the mystery of mortal beauty. What was it? That is to say, what was it when you could not define it, when you could enumerate no special outstanding attributes? When you could point to speaking eyes and chiselled features, majesty, perfect proportions, exquisite finish, it was simple enough. If Bertrand had seen Zita's sisters, he would have had no difficulty in defining their quality and pointing out their assets and what was lacking. But here there were none of these things in a high enough degree to account for the whole effect. There were no obvious assets: soft eyes, yes; a well-cut face, a good line, a charming expression…and yet you looked, he did, an artist, that is to say…spellbound. He could not take his eyes off her. There was nothing marvellous, no obvious perfection, and yet there was something in the whole of her appearance, something that emanated from her texture, line, movement and expression like a phrase of music, or the light on a cloud, or the unexpected sight of a branch of blossom, or the sudden scent of a hyacinth, something in the *substance* beyond the accidents of flesh and bone, shape and colour; and that substance was celestial.

'She is beautiful. Yes,' thought Bertrand, 'but what is her impalpable quality, that is, as it were, outside beauty and beyond it?'

He asked her how she would like to be painted.

"Just as you like," she said. "Paint me just as I am. Only I suppose I had better take off my hat?"

"Why?" said Bertrand.

"It will be out of fashion next year," she said.

She was wearing a small straw bonnet tied under her chin with a black ribbon.

"It is a great mistake," said Bertrand, "to be afraid of the fashion when one is painting a portrait, or to try and neutralize it. Nothing dates so quickly and so sharply as fancy dress, and when people have their portraits painted and try to make the clothes of the day look of no date, but as much as possible like fancy dress, the picture dates quicker than one which accepts the fashion and doesn't mind; the hair always betrays the date, even when the model is dressed as Cleopatra or Mary Stuart."

"I expect you know best," said Zita. "Paint me just as you like, but without my bonnet."

"Just as you are," Bertrand said, laughing, "but with the bonnet, a profile. It will be perfect. I promise you in ten years' time your coiffure will have become far more old-fashioned than your hat."

"Very well," said Zita, with a sigh, "with the bonnet."

And so the sittings began. And with the sittings began a new life for Zita. Bertrand did not talk much while he worked, but he talked unlike anyone she had met hitherto. He was a slow worker, and Zita did not make him feel inclined to work faster. They talked on general topics, and the more often Bertrand saw Zita the less he felt he knew her: she was so young, and yet she seemed so old for her age; so inexperienced and yet (so he felt) disillusioned, with possibilities of gaiety all locked up in a box.

And then she seemed so utterly aloof; to know nobody, either here in Paris or in England; and she talked of her mother and of her sisters as if they belonged to another world.

Bertrand was married and he told his wife about this strange Englishwoman who was so unlike any of the Englishwomen he had ever seen or heard of. One evening Bertrand and his wife received a visit from his wife's brother, Jean de Bosis, who stayed to dinner. Jean de Bosis was only twenty-seven years old. He had literary ambitions and had written some verse; some of it had been printed in reviews, but as yet he had not published a book. Jean asked Bertrand whether he was busy.

"I am doing a portrait of an English lady."

"What is an Englishwoman doing in Paris at this time of year?" asked Jean.

"She is living here: her husband is in a bank. They stay here all the summer and take their holiday in autumn or winter, not to miss some kind of sport – I forget which."

"I see," said Jean, "she is sportive."

"Not at all. It is her husband, who is much older than she is."

"Then she is young and pretty?"

"Young, yes; pretty is not the word. She is…she is interesting to paint…and difficult – very difficult."

"Is she one of those Englishwomen who are as tall as poles and flat as boards?"

"No, she is not like that. She looks to me like a flower that is pining for want of sunlight."

"What flower?" asked Jean.

"A branch of lilac," he said, "but on a day when there isno sun. If there were only sunlight, one feels she would be dazzling. That is by the way. I don't know what she will suggest to you, but to me she is like something dazzling that for the moment is undergoing a soft eclipse."

"Perhaps she is like the Sleeping Beauty in the wood?"

"Perhaps; I don't think so. I think she is wide-awake, so wide-awake that she can never get to sleep; but if you would like to see her, all you have to do is to come to my studio tomorrow between ten and twelve – she will be there."

"And the husband?"

"An Englishman…clean and sensible – likes racing."

"He loves his wife?"

"He would be capable of being jealous – he wouldn't be easy."

"Does he come with her?"

"He brings her always, but he never stays."

The next morning – it was a hot morning in July – Jean de Bosis went to Bertrand's studio. He found Bertrand hard at work painting Mrs Harmer. She was dressed in muslin and wearing her little straw bonnet.

"Talk as much as you like," Bertrand said, after he had introduced them, "but forgive me if I am rude and absent-minded. I am in the middle of something difficult."

Jean sat down. Zita seemed to be interested in him at once; his features were a little rough: his eyes, dark and grey and trustful, and full of understanding and gentleness. They were talking of people going away, of the heat, the crowd.

"Personally, I like Paris in July, one feels so much freer," he said.

"I used to feel like that in London in August, when it was supposed to be empty. It was just as full really, only the five or six people you *didn't* want to see were away, and that made all the difference."

"That's just it," said Jean. "You miss London, madame?"

"Oh, no. I lived in London very little after I was grown up – only a month. My husband lived in the country, and my mother lives abroad."

"The English country is so lovely," said Jean.

"You know it?"

"Only from Bertrand's descriptions and from books."

"You speak English?"

"Not at all, and I only read English books in translation. But I have read Shakespeare, Byron, Dickens and Ouida. You are a great reader, madame?"

"I read novels, and I forget them."

"French novels?" asked Jean.

"French, English, and even Russian novels translated – Tauchnitz, mostly. It passes the time."

"You must be homesick for England."

"Not at all," Zita smiled. "I like Paris and I like French people; they are so civil, and then they notice that one exists."

"Did you escape notice in England?" Jean asked, with an accent of good-humoured irony. "That would, I think, be difficult to believe."

"But it is true, nevertheless."

"English people must be very absent-minded."

As he said this he looked at her with such undisguised admiration that she felt shy and blushed.

"Do you read novels?" she said, to change the subject.

"I have read all the novels everyone has read. One has to do that once, and then one need never do it again."

"Jean de Bosis is a poet," said Bertrand. "He has published

sonnets in the *Revue Blanche*."

"That is the sad truth," said Jean.

"Why sad?" asked Zita.

"Because if they had been really good they would have been refused."

"They were accepted," said Bertrand, "because they prove that he has something in him: whether he will write verse or not, is another affair. I am sure he will write something."

"I often wonder," said Jean, taking no notice of what Bertrand had said, "whether things in life ever happen as they do in a novel. Do you think they do?"

"When you are reading a novel," said Bertrand, "you oughtn't to feel it has really happened. A novel must not be too lifelike, or else where does the artist come in?"

"If a writer," said Jean, "invents a whole story and means you to think it like life, and you *do* think it like life, I consider he is a good artist. But life seems to me so badly constructed, as if the author were constantly forgetting what he had meant his characters to do."

"He never forgets what he means his characters to be," said Bertrand; "people remain themselves."

"I don't agree," said Jean. "I think people are continually changing. They say that every seven years one has a totally new body. I am quite certain that every seven years one has a totally new mind. One has become a different person. And thinkof one's friends. Every seven years one wants a new set of friends."

Bertrand laughed.

"What are you laughing at?" asked Jean.

"I was wondering how you could possibly know. Seven years ago you were a schoolboy."

"I wasn't; I was a soldier. I don't have to wait seven years to change," said Jean. "I can't look at the books I adored three years ago."

"And the people?" asked Zita.

21

"Oh people – people are all alike. The more they change the more they stay the same."

"That's exactly what I said just now, and what you contradicted," said Bertrand.

"I meant, we always see the same people here, we never see anything new, different, never hear anything original, fresh, except ..." he stopped.

"Except when?" asked Zita.

"I stopped just in time; I was just going to pay you a banal compliment, madame, and then I remembered that English people don't like compliments."

"Don't they?" asked Zita, with serious expression. Jean laughed.

"Why are you laughing?" she asked.

"It is you who are laughing at me."

"Oh! No! I assure you."

"Bertrand," said Jean, "you should paint Madame Harmer just as she was just now, when she laughed at me with her serious face; it would be marvellous. May I see?"

He walked towards the easel.

"No, not yet, wait till the end of the sitting. I shall not be a moment. I have done all I can today. There is little more I can do at all. The truth is, madame, you are too difficult – no, painters don't pay compliments. There is something intangible; it is as if there were a curtain of gauze between you and the world, and then every day you are different. But it is more than that. It was as if you had the gift of making yourself almost invisible; of closing your petals. I feel there is something to see which I could paint, but you will not let me see it. You are wearing an invisible mask; or perhaps it is that I don't know how to paint – how to look. What a trade! There now, I've finished for today."

"May we look?" asked Zita.

"Yes, you may look now." He walked back himself and looked at the canvas critically.

"It seems to me wonderfully painted," said Zita; "of course I can't judge."

"Yes," said Jean, "it's good; it's very good; *mais il y a quelque chose qui manque*, the touch of mockery, the malice."

"Ah! that was not there last time," said Bertrand.

"You think I am mischievous, wicked?" asked Zita.

"Not wicked, but I think if you liked you could be very – "

"Very what?"

But at that moment Bertrand's servant announced that monsieur was awaiting madame below.

# CHAPTER IV

The sittings went on for a month, and Jean de Bosis attended them often, but the picture did not seem to advance. These sittings made a great difference to Zita's life: they brought something new into it, and something gay.

Zita never met either Bertrand or Jean de Bosis anywhere except at the studio, and this situation might have continued unchanged but for the arrival of Legge's wife, Amelia. She arrived, although the apartment was not ready, feeling that if she did not come it never would be ready. Perhaps she was right.

Amelia Legge was not pretty, but everybody said she had a nice face. She arrived in Paris with her two little boys…shewas only just over thirty; practical, shrill, plaintive, energetic, shrewd, inquisitive, and brimming with human interest. She stayed at an hotel one day only; the next day she and her husband moved into their apartment which, although it looked then as if it could not be finished for months, was, after they had once got into it, practically finished in forty-eight hours.

They dined together on the night of their arrival, at their favourite restaurant out of doors, near the Rond Point. And they had hardly finished their melon when Amelia said: "Fancy Robert being here!"

"Yes," said Legge, "and established for good, at least I suppose for the next four or five years, or perhaps for ever; he's a partner in the Bristol Bank. But what really interests me is his wife; what is she? I asked the young men in the Chancery, and all they know is that she has been here since the summer before last. He goes to the races regularly, and she goes *nowhere*."

"Well," said Amelia, "if I may say a word, darling, I can tell you quite a lot about her. In the first place, she is Teresa St Alwyn's sister."

"I know, your cousin told me that."

"The youngest. Robert met her at Nice. They were married the year before we were married, and then they went to England and lived, I think, in the country, at Robert's house, Wallington, near Easthampton, a dreadful place, a regular 'Bleak House'. She's good-looking, but nothing like so good-looking as the sisters, so they say."

"Well, I'm not sure you're right," said Legge. "Bertrand says she's a dream."

"Artists!" said Amelia, "they always admire what other people don't admire. They like discovering something nobody else sees; in fact, they like what they can paint."

"But he says she's unpaintable."

"You haven't seen her?"

"No. I left cards, but your cousin made it plain he didn't want to do anything till you came."

"Poor child; she must be lonely," said Amelia. "But we will change all that; I've written to Robert already."

Two days later Robert asked the Legges to luncheon.

"Amelia would like," he explained to his wife, "a lot of jabbering Frenchmen to meet her, but she won't get that here."

"I think she sounds rather alarming," said Zita.

"No," said Robert, "Amelia's all right really; she's a sensible woman, but she's restless, and she likes to have a finger in every pie."

She arrived the next day at one. She was unlike what Zita had expected. Zita had expected something gaunt and spare, and tall and hard; Amelia Legge was soft and fair, essentially comfortable. She was warm in her manner. Cyril Legge was affable, buoyant and gay. Amelia greeted Robert affectionately, and then said: "So this is Zita. I used to know your mother a little. You are like her and like your beautiful sisters. You didn't tell me, Robert, she was the most beautiful of the lot. I remember your elder sister, Teresa, coming out; it was the year I came out; she made a sensation, but there…"

There was not a shadow of doubt that Amelia admired Zita. The Suttons and Wilmot, his partner, whom Robert had asked, arrived, and they went in to luncheon.

Sutton asked after the portrait, and Zita said it had been almost finished when Bertrand had painted out everything he had done and started afresh.

"I must see it at once, dear," said Amelia, "I admire Bertrand's work *enormously*."

"I've got a sitting tomorrow," said Zita, "if you would like to come."

"I should like it above all things."

"Then you can bring Zita back," said Robert, "and have luncheon with us."

"Does Robert always take you to and from the studio?" asked Amelia.

"Always to," said Zita, "and sometimes from."

"He's damned slow painting the thing," said Harmer; "nearly a month now, and he's hardly begun."

"Bertrand is always like that," said Sutton. "He is a slow starter; he'll work for six weeks and throw away everything he has done, then start again and finish it off in forty-eight hours."

"I hope it will be worth looking at when it's finished," said Harmer. "I wish we could have had it done in London by Millais, or someone like that."

"You're lucky to have got Bertrand," said Amelia; "you will never regret it."

They talked of other things. When the party broke up Amelia

stayed behind with Zita.

"You must tell me at once," she said, "when you want to get rid of me, but as I am Robert's cousin and have known your sister, I can't feel that you are a stranger."

Zita thought Amelia original, lively, and comfortable. On the other hand she did not feel that anybody so intensely interested in human nature and in other people's affairs as Amelia obviously was, could help being indiscreet.

Amelia spoke a great deal of Paris, the Paris that she had known as a child, and that was now so changed, but where she still had a great many old friends – friends of her parents.

After asking Zita whether she knew so-and-so and so-and-so, Amelia realized that Zita knew no French people at all.

"So you know no French people?" she said.

"Not one, except Mr Bertrand who is painting me, and there is another man who has been once or twice while I have been sitting."

"Who's that?" asked Amelia.

"His name is Jean de Bosis; he writes."

"I will ask Madeleine if she knows him. You must know Madeleine Laurent, she is a great friend of mine. She doesn't write herself, but she knows all the writers. She likes English people, too – sincerely. She has even been to England, once. Fancy Bertrand painting you! Whoever put that into Robert's head? Robert's a dear, and I'm devoted to him, but the arts are not his strong point."

"It was Mr Sutton who suggested it," said Zita, "and your husband approved."

"I suppose you've been to the Embassy?"

"We went to a garden-party."

"But, my dear child, why live like a hermit? Why not make friends?"

"Foreigners bore Robert," said Zita, "and I am rather shy too. I am quite happy as I am."

"Seeing no one; going nowhere?"

"I see a great deal of Robert's English friends." Amelia Legge needed to hear nothing further. She divined the tenor of Zita's life with perfect accuracy. And she was appalled.

"Unless something is done," she said to herself, "this will end in disaster." And Amelia Legge was one of those people who, when they resolve that a thing is to be done, set about to do it.

She drove back to her apartment. She wrote a few letters and then drove to keep an appointment with her friend, Madeleine Laurent. Madeleine Laurent lived in a small apartment in a street leading into one of the new avenues. She was expecting Amelia Legge, and greeted her warmly with a wealth of kisses and exclamations. They each gushed at each other for a time. They both had warm, expansive, exuberant natures. Madeleine Laurent was a widow. In her youth she had done a little professional painting, but now she had given it up. Her husband had been dead some years. She lived for her friends, of whom she had a great number, both in France and England.

She was small, dark, but not at all semitic-looking; her nose turned up a little; her eyes were full of observation and fun. There was something electric about her, but the electricity was in her expression; her movements were calm and rare.

She led Amelia to a divan in a room almost entirely furnished with high bookcases and without pictures, except the portrait of a man on an easel, and bombarded her with pertinent questions. She commented briefly, sometimes only by a nod of the head, on Amelia's answers.

"I've found a cousin here," said Amelia, "who is married."

"What cousin is that?"

"Nobody, my dear, you would know, a middle-aged *homme d'affaires*; but the point is he has now married the daughter of people I knew, a girl whom I had never set eyes on till yesterday, and she's a real beauty, and charming."

"*Quel genre?*" asked Madame Laurent.

"I don't know. I have never seen anybody like her. You would notice her anywhere. She has got a lovely smile and wide apart eyes; but she is celestial – like a tune played on muted strings or on a piano with the sourdine."

"Tall?"

"Not really, I think, but she made me feel even smaller than I am."

"And how long have they been married?"

"Seven years."

"Then she is much younger than her husband?"

"Oh, much; she is only about twenty-seven."

"And children?"

"There was one – stillborn. She can have no more."

"And any *roman*?"

"Ah, that I don't know. It is the first time I have seen her. I know Robert, her husband, very well. Apart from his being my first cousin and having known him all my life, we have always been great friends. I like Robert immensely and I admire him. I think he is remarkable in many ways besides being, everyone says, a first-rate man of business. I'm not surprised at his being attracted by a girl like that, but I do rather wonder whether it was wise to marry someone so much younger than himself and so different."

"So different?"

"Oh! yes. One can see that at a glance. You see my cousin is a North countryman, shrewd and practical, fond of outdoor life and sports, but quite capable of giving them up for a time if necessary; fond of horses and racing, but all the artistic side of life – art, literature, music, painting – is a sealed book to him."

"And she?"

"Ah, she…I don't know what she likes, but nothing could be more different. She was brought up in a convent, and when the father died they lived at Cannes and Nice, anywhere, in pensions; so you see. I suppose she must have been in love with Robert to have married him. I don't know what she's really like, nor what she thinks, but I'm certain of one thing, that between her and Robert there cannot be one idea in common. I knew her mother – a sensible, amusing American, who they say was a beauty; and her father, a charming adventurer, half Irish, and cosmopolitan. The sisters were beautiful, and they married, but I think Zita is the best-looking of all of them. She is being painted here."

"Who by?"

"Bertrand."

"Ah!"

"And, by the way, there is a man apparently who goes to the studio to look on, Jean de Bosis. Do you know him?"

"Yes, I know him well. His mother is my greatest friend."

"He will be able to tell you all about Zita Harmer. But I shall soon know more myself; in the meantime, can I bring her to see you?"

"Of course; bring her tomorrow, it's my *jour*. Does she like seeing people?"

"I think she might, but I don't believe my poor cousin has ever given her the opportunity. You see he goes to the races, and he never asks anyone to the house except business friends."

"Is he jealous?"

"That would be the obvious explanation, and had occurred even to me."

Madeleine laughed.

"But, but," Amelia went on, "I don't think it's the right one after all."

"No?"

"Well, you see Robert is in many ways an odd man, and it's quite possible he may be jealous of *everybody*, but he's very *fair*, and I am quite certain he is not jealous of *anyone*."

# CHAPTER V

The next morning Amelia Legge went with Zita to the studio. Mrs Legge admired the picture, and she made the acquaintance of Jean de Bosis, who was there as usual. She took Zita in the afternoon to see Madeleine Laurent. There were not more than four or five people there – there never were. Madeleine Laurent took an instant fancy to Zita and admired her.

"She is a *belle de nuit*," she said to Amelia.

The arrival of the Legges entirely changed Zita's life. Cyril Legge's apartment soon became an agreeable centre of a group of literary and artistic people, French, English and foreign. They asked Zita and Robert as often as they could to their house, and at first it was not difficult to get them to come, but Robert suddenly urged Zita to go without him to the Legges. He distrusted foreigners, it is true, but he thought she was safe among the literary, and just at that time he made friends with a handsome American widow, a Mrs Rylands, who was to play an important part in his life. She was about the same age as himself – a practical, sensible woman of great and ripe experience. It was thought by some to be a liaison, by others not. Robert Harmer admired her immensely and took everything she said for gospel. He found it more and more convenient for Zita to go out by herself to houses of intimate friends.

Bertrand finished his picture, and it was exhibited inthe

spring at the Salon. It attracted a great deal of attention. It was the year of the Exhibition. There were many foreigners and many English people in Paris. Cyril Legge had persuaded Robert, without difficulty, to go to the Embassy, and the English people who saw Zita there, hearing her picture, *Portrait de Madame* — talked about, and behaving, as usual, like sheep, began to admire her, having said before, without having seen her, that she could not hold a candle to any of her sisters; the catchword which was now handed about was that she was the best-looking of the whole family.

She had certainly blossomed into something ravishing. She was lovely because she was happy, and she was happy because she was admired. That spring and summer, Sarah Bernhardt, who had just appeared as Doña Sol in *Hernani*, and Zita and her portrait were the two main topics. But it was neither the catchwords of the fashionable nor the admiration of the man-in-the-street that affected Zita, but the admiration of one person: Jean de Bosis.

And now I come to the moment of the story when Amelia Legge says she was probably to blame, although she never was prepared to plead guilty. The facts are these: when Bertrand finished his picture, Zita could, of course, no longer see Jean de Bosis at the studio. At first the only place where they met was Madeleine Laurent's, where there were seldom less than four other people. Zita never asked him to her apartment, and Madeleine Laurent was not at home to visitors except on her day. By this time Zita had got to know Mrs Legge intimately; intimately for her, that is to say. Zita was not a person who allowed people to become intimate with her; she was veiled and reserved, and generally rather silent. Amelia thought her a puzzle. She liked her immensely, but she did not pretend to understand her. She was startled sometimes by the things that Zita would say. For instance, one day they were talking of her sister, Teresa, and Zita said she thought she was one of the most fortunate people in the world. Amelia asked why, and Zita said she was fortunate because if her husband hadn't left her she would have led a miserable life; she simply hated wealth and everything that appertained to it. Now Amelia thought she knew Teresa well. She had known her as a girl, and met her since her separation at Rome, where Teresa had stayed at the Embassy, and she knew that Teresa detested poverty and moreover felt lonely; that she had been devoted to her husband in spite of all; also that she was extravagant, pleasure-loving, and born with expensive tastes, which she was obliged to forgo, and she made no secret of this. But Amelia reflected that people rarely understood their brothers and sisters; they knew them too well and not well enough.

Then there was another occasion; Zita and Robert were to dine with the Legges one evening, and the day before Amelia, in reminding Zita of it, said: "By the way (Amelia was greedy and knew all about cooking), does Robert like langouste, or can't he eat it?"

"Oh!" said Zita, "Robert likes anything. He doesn't know what he is eating."

This remark opened a door for Amelia on all sorts of things, and it amazed her, or rather it puzzled her more than ever – as Robert had told her that he ordered dinner himself and saw to all that…and indeed the food at the Harmers' flat was delicious; and did Zita think that it all came from heaven by accident, or was entirely the doing of the cook, who had been engaged by Robert, so he said, after a thorough investigation and a searching cross-examination, and a great deal of trouble? It also threw light on Robert and his behaviour to Zita. It was obvious that he never made any fuss about any domestic or kitchen details, and Amelia, who knew how particular he was, thought that he deserved credit. It amazed her that Zita should be so blind, but then she reflected – perhaps women are blind when their husbands are concerned. Or was she wrong? Was Robert blind? Were they both blind and was Zita right?

Did Zita really do everything?

Another time they were discussing a common acquaintance, Hedworth Lawless, who was at that time Minister at Copenhagen and was staying in Paris on his way through. Hedworth Lawless was good-looking and was thought to be a great charmer; they were talking of him and Zita said: "Lady Lawless is so sensible, she is never jealous; I suppose she thinks there's safety in numbers." Now Amelia knew that so far from its being a question of numbers, there was only one person who counted in Hedworth Lawless's life, an Italian who had married a diplomat, and that, so far from not being jealous, Lady Lawless would have been jealous even had she ceased to love; she would have had toothache even after losing all her teeth. Then she reflected – Lady Lawless is a clever woman, and Zita is ingenuous. But when one day, talking of Jean de Bosis, Zita said she thought he had an essentially happy nature; that he was entirely domestic, devoted to his mother; that he would marry, have a large family and not stir from his fireside, his garden and his farm in Normandy, then Amelia said to herself: "Zita isn't stupid, but she has no more perception than a rhinoceros, which is curious, considering what a sensitive creature she is in some ways." And the more she saw of her and the better she got to know her, the more she was convinced that this was the truth.

"Zita is either unperceptive or deep," she said to Madeleine Laurent.

"Oh," said Madeleine, "she is deep, but not in the sense you mean: she could be a well of suffering, and it is partly because she is unperceptive. Any French person could see she is unperceptive at once. *Elle ne sait pas même s'arranger.* Which for a woman with her beauty is a pity."

But to get back to why Amelia thought herself to blame; Zita had got into the habit of dropping into the Legges' apartment at any time; and the visits of Jean de Bosis began to be more frequent. Cyril Legge liked him and always pressed his wife to invite him, which she did, seeing no reason why she shouldn't.

At first Robert used to come with his wife, but as his intimacy with Mrs Rylands increased and it became a matter of seeing her every day, he found it more convenient to let Zita go out by herself.

Then Zita started having a day. Jean de Bosis used to attend it regularly. Sometimes he would stay a little while after the other guests had gone. Zita would sometimes ask him to dinner. Things went on like this till the spring of the next year, and Amelia was unaware of there being anything unusualor perilous in the situation until some of those little things happened that leave you perplexed and guessing, and not a little uneasy; little incidents that give one the tantalizing feeling that the right key is in the lock and just about to be turned, and yet cannot be turned, or that there is a rift in the firmamentand that you could look through the clouds and see what you want to see, only it closes again too soon.

Two little incidents of this nature occurred.

This was the first.

The Legges arranged a small party one night to go to the Théâtre français. There was a revival of *Ruy Blas*; Sarah Bernhardt was playing the part of the Queen of Spain. Cyril had taken a box, one of those boxes in which people sit in twos: two in front, then two behind, and then two behind those. The party consisted of the Legges, Bertrand and his wife, Jean de Bosis and Zita. Robert had dined with the Legges on condition that he might be spared a play in verse.

In the box the party was arranged like this: Madame Bertrand and Zita were in front – Zita on the side of the box nearest to the stage; then Amelia and Bertrand, and then Jean de Bosis and Legge. Jean was on the extreme left, at the greatest distance from Zita, so that she could see him, and he, looking at the stage, could look straight at her.

When Sarah Bernhardt came to the lines:

'Qui que tu sois, ami dont l'ombre m'accompagne,

Puisque mon cœur subit une inflexible loi,
Sois aimé par ta mère et sois béni par moi!'

which she sighed like an Aeolian harp, Zita, who was looking at
the stage and had tears in her eyes, turned her head in the
direction of Jean de Bosis. You could not have said their eyes
had met, because she had turned her head back and he was
looking at the stage once more. It happened in a second; it was
a mere nothing; and yet Amelia noticed it, and in noting it she
felt that something electric and significant had brushed past
her.

During the entr'acte they walked in the foyer. Zita walked
arm in arm with Bertrand and Amelia with Jean de Bosis. Jean
discussed the play with Amelia and said it needed a genius to
make one swallow so absurd a story: "but, after all," he said,
"the plots of all the greatest plays are absurd. It is absurd to
think Oedipus could have lived for twelve years without
mentioning the past; that, after being told he was to kill his
father and marry his mother, he should have killed an old man
and married a woman much older than himself without
suspecting anything might be wrong, is frankly incredible. But
I am ready to accept the *donnée* of any story the dramatist
likes to set before me on condition of not thinking it out. What
could be sillier than the plot of *King Lear*? What could be
more wildly improbable than the conduct of Othello? *Ruy
Blas* isn't a sillier story than any of these, and it is dramatic,
and Sarah Bernhardt makes the queen seem as true as
Desdemona or Cordelia." Cordelia somehow or other made
Amelia think of Zita, because she felt that Zita might have
behaved like Cordelia, but she couldn't have behaved like
Desdemona.

"Bertrand," she said, "told me at dinner that he wants to
paint another picture of Zita; what do you think?"

"He can always try," said Jean, "but nobody but Velasquez
could have painted her."

"Velasquez?" said Amelia, surprised.

"Yes, because of the small head," he said, pensively.

That was the second of the little things. Amelia wondered. When the play was over the Legges dropped Zita at her apartment.

On the way they talked about the play and the acting.

"Bertrand wants to paint you again," said Amelia, "but Jean de Bosis says there is only one painter who could have painted you, Velasquez!"

"Velasquez!" said Zita, with a slightly artificial laugh. "What an idea! I wonder what made him think that?"

"He thought that," said Amelia, "because you have got such a small head."

Zita said nothing, but Amelia thought in the darkness that Zita had blushed, and she wondered once more. She was left guessing.

# CHAPTER VI

In the month of August that year Robert took a moor in
Scotland in the same remote spot in the north. He asked some
of his friends, the only other woman besides Zita being Flora
Sutton. He asked Mrs Rylands but she had been ordered by the
doctors to take waters. He asked the Legges, but Cyril could
not leave Paris. The Legges stayed in Paris all through August
and September. Jean de Bosis went to stay with his mother in
Normandy. But he came to Paris often, and every time he came
he visited the Legges and talked about Zita. When the Harmers
came back from Scotland, Bertrand asked permission to paint
Zita again, this time for himself. Robert was delighted. Bertrand
painted her in an evening gown this time: cream-coloured satin
and tulle, with a tea rose near her heart. The picture is now in
the Luxembourg, and is thought to be Bertrand's masterpiece.
Amelia went often to the sittings now; Jean de Bosis suddenly
gave up going altogether, nor did he any longer pay visits to the
Legges; nor was he seen at Zita's day – he had disappeared.

Amelia mentioned his name one day to Zita and she said:

"We never see him now at all. I think he is living in the
country with his mother."

Talking it over with her husband, Amelia said to him:

"I believe I was wrong after all about Zita and Jean de
Bosis."

"Yes?"

"I don't believe she cares for him, and he never goes to the studio now, or here, as to that, and he never goes near Zita."

"I expect he found it was useless," said Cyril. "Or perhaps Robert noticed it?"

"No," said Amelia, decisively, "Robert could never be jealous of a Frenchman. As far as Zita is concerned, he thinks foreigners don't count. In his eyes they belong to a different category. He could never imagine Zita being attracted by a foreigner."

"But supposing," said Legge, "cousin Robert knew for certain Zita was attracted by a foreigner, what then?"

"Ah! then I don't know."

It was in the spring, shortly after the opening of the Salon, when everyone was talking of Bertrand's new picture, and the English people in Paris were raving about Zita's portrait, and Robert seemed to be enjoying their admiration, that Jean de Bosis published his first book, a small book of verse called *Stances*. It attracted little attention and few copies of it were sold.

Amelia heard of the publication from Madeleine, who was interested.

"He is not a poet," she said to Amelia, as they sat together late one afternoon in Madeleine's flat, the day of her *jour*, when the visitors had gone, "but he has got talent certainly, and I expect he will write something, but not verse."

"Are there any love poems in it?" asked Amelia, who was interested more in the personal than in the artistic side of poetry.

"No," said Madeleine, "nature poems and landscapes. There are one or two love poems – the wreaths on the already faded tomb of a dead love. He was unlucky for the time being."

"Why unlucky?"

"He loved someone who didn't love him and who never could love him?"

"Zita?"

"Yes."

"You think she didn't – doesn't?"

"I am sure."

"And he?"

"Oh, he *did*…but when he saw it was useless, that there was nothing to be done, he gave it up."

"It is all over then?"

"It has been over for a long time now. There are only a few pale reflections of it in the book. There it is, you can take it if you like. Jean has been in the country getting over it. It was like a bad illness, but it is all over now, and soon it will be someone else. He has a *coeur à louer* and it will not stay long vacant."

"Has it always been occupied before?"

"Always more or less, but never by anyone who mattered – till this."

"This was serious, you think?"

"Very. He took it badly."

"And she?"

"She was quite indifferent."

"You think she is – "

"*Un glaçon*, yes."

"Well, I don't believe she was ever in love with Robert."

"Of course not."

"But her mother – "

"Her mother – that was *autre chose*. Her mother was nothing but temperament."

Amelia sighed.

"It's just as well," said Madeleine.

"What?"

"Well, that nothing happened."

"I suppose so. May I take this book?"

"Do. You will see he has talent."

Amelia took the book home with her. She opened it and chanced on a poem about ploughed fields, and then on another about autumn woods and ponds, and felt she had read enough.

Had she read the book more carefully she would have come across a poem that might have interested her. It was called 'L'Exilé', and it told of a lovely princess with a small head, and of the hopeless passion she inspired in the heart of an alien wayfarer.

That evening the Legges dined with Robert and Zita. The first thing that Amelia noticed on one of the small tables when she arrived was Jean de Bosis' poems with a written dedication on the cover.

"Have you read Jean de Bosis' poems?" she asked Zita.

"He sent them to me," she said; "so kind of him, but I don't really care for French poetry. It's to me like oil poured on smooth water."

Robert, who was listening, took up the book and glanced at it, cut a few pages with a paper-cutter, and put it down again.

After dinner there was music. Flora Sutton sang some English sentimental songs – English ballads with tunes by Tosti, and Legge, who had a pleasing baritone, sang some Schumann. Robert, who was not musical, sat in the corner of the room near the table, and Amelia noticed that he took up Jean de Bosis' poems and read them as if absorbed. She wondered how much he understood of them. Not much, she thought; but perhaps he enjoyed the poem about the wild ducks in the dawn. He was a lover of nature, if inarticulate.

The guests went away early. Zita and Robert were left alone. Robert lit a cigar.

"That fellow writes quite well," said Robert, after a time.

"Who?" asked Zita.

"Bosis." (Robert pronounced the word 'Bossis'.)

Zita said nothing.

"He describes wild duck getting up from a marsh very well."

"I haven't had time to read them yet," said Zita. "I must read them soon."

"You must be quick if you want to read them before we go

away."

"Are we going away?" said Zita.

"Yes," said Robert, with a sigh, as of infinite relief, "for good. They want me in London."

"When did you settle this?"

"I heard from our people in London this morning, but I didn't make up my mind till this evening."

"Oh!" said Zita.

"Do you mind?"

"Oh no, of course not. I shall be sorry to go in some ways. We shall miss the Legges."

"Yes, we shall miss the Legges."

There was a long pause. It was broken by Zita, who said:

"Where shall we live in England?"

"At Wallington, as soon as the tenant goes."

"Just as before?"

"Yes, just as before."

"And how soon shall we go?"

"Tomorrow fortnight, but I am going over to London the day after tomorrow for two days."

"I see. I am sleepy," said Zita, "I am going to bed."

"I am not going to bed yet. I have a letter to write. Good night, my dear."

"Good night, Robert."

As Zita went through the little antechamber into her bedroom, she saw a letter for her on the table. She opened it. It was from Madame Bertrand. They had asked a few friends to come to the studio the next afternoon between five and seven. If they were doing nothing better and happened to be anywhere near, she would meet some friends – Madeleine Laurent, and they were asking the Legges. There would be a little music … etc.

Zita went to bed and stayed awake a long time after she heard Robert go to bed. She was thinking of Wallington.

Next day Zita went to the studio with Madeleine Laurent. Robert had encouraged her to go but would not take her himself, because he could not stand musical parties in a studio, and as he was starting for London the next morning he wanted to have tea with Mrs Rylands. The Legges were not at the studio, there were only French people there; among others Jean de Bosis. Zita thanked him for sending her his book, and told him they – she and her husband – were leaving Paris.

"For a while?" he asked.

"No, for good," she said, looking straight in front of her at a large unfinished picture on the wall at the other end of the room.

"To London?" he asked.

"No, not to London; at least, my husband will be a lot in London, but I shall be in the country."

"And how soon?"

Zita told him what had been arranged, and then their conversation was interrupted, as someone began to sing – a contralto. She sang a song of Godard's.

Zita had no further talk with Jean, but the Bertrands heard the news of her coming departure, and were loud in their regrets. Robert started for London the next morning.

"I shall be back in three days," he said. "I have written to Amelia and told her to look after you."

"But I'm coming with you to the station," said Zita.

"No, don't bother," said Robert. "I hate goodbyes at stations, and there won't be time."

"But I'm ready," said Zita. She had on her hat. "I am quite ready."

"No, dear," said Robert. "I would rather you didn't come."

"Very well," she said.

This was the first time she had not accompanied him to the station. It is true he had seldom gone away by himself.

Robert then said goodbye to Zita and left at once. He liked

being in good time for the train.

"You'll have a long time to wait," Zita said, looking at the clock.

"I don't mind waiting, and I hate being rushed."

He had been gone about five minutes when a clerk from the bank arrived, much flustered, saying he had brought an important letter for M. Harmer, which it was essential he should take with him to London. He had been delayed and he had not thought M. Harmer would have started so soon, but, no matter, he would go straight to the station.

"I shall have time to catch him," he said.

"I will take it," said Zita; "there is something I have forgotten to tell him." She had still got on her hat.

She took the letter from the slightly reluctant clerk, and rang for a fiacre.

She arrived at the Gare du Nord in plenty of time. She caught sight of Robert standing on the platform smoking a cigar. He was surprised to see her. She told him what had happened, and gave him the letter.

"And I forgot to tell you I want you to bring me back a cake of spermaceti soap. This is where you can get it."

She gave him a piece of paper. He kissed her and said goodbye. There was still nearly ten minutes before the train was to start, but she thought it would irritate him if she stayed. As she walked down the platform she met Mrs Rylands arriving with a lot of hand luggage and engaged in voluble explanations to a porter and a maid. When she saw Zita she stopped.

"I'm going to London," she said, "by the same train as your husband. I'm going to see about getting a house. My niece whom I'm looking after is bent on living in London."

"You'll find Robert further up," said Zita, "we have said goodbye, and I must go home."

They said goodbye amicably. Zita drove back to her apartment in a fiacre.

It was a lovely May morning; the chestnuts were in flower. Paris was radiant and gay.

Zita was not jealous of Mrs Rylands, but it irritated her that her husband should treat Mrs Rylands with reverence. It irritated her that he had said nothing about her going to London, although she had heard she was going to London some time or other. When she got home she found a letter waiting for her on the table of the antechamber. She recognized the handwriting at once. It was from Jean de Bosis. So far she had only received brief notes from him, and these rarely – answers to invitations. This was a long letter – eight pages and more – in his sloping, clear and sensitive handwriting. It turned out to be longer than she had thought, more than eight pages. After reading the first page she sat down in an armchair. It was a love-letter, a declaration. He told her that he had always worshipped her from the very first moment he had seen her, but had not dared say anything; he just thought it hopeless. He had believed in her profound indifference. But gradually he had begun to have hopes. He had thought, after the night they went to *Ruy Blas*, that she cared a little. When she had left Paris for Scotland this last time he had nearly gone mad. Never had he been through anything like that. Never had he known a man could suffer what he had suffered. Then, when she came back, he thought she was so little pleased to see him that everything he had dreamt about her feelings had been a mistake: he was certain she did not care for him. He decided to go away. He would cure himself. He had ambitions – he wanted to be a poet, to do something with his life, to be someone; why should he waste his life, throw it away for someone who did not even know whether he was alive or dead? Then that day when they had met at Bertrand's studio and she had said she was going away for good, he knew that he had looked into her soul and read the secret of her heart. She *did* care; she *did* mind going. She was unhappy. She was more than unhappy. She was desperate. He knew now that she loved him.

He understood what she was feeling and what her life would be if she went to England with her husband now. He had a practical plan to suggest. She should leave her husband and go with him to Algiers. He had a little house there; it was all ready waiting; he was independent; they would have plenty to live on.

He knew she loved him as much as he loved her. Why should she sacrifice herself? What for? and for whom? She would have no remorse about her husband. She knew only too well that he was fully occupied. When they got tired of Algiers they would go elsewhere. Would she mind the *qu'en dira-t-on*? He thought not. If they loved each other, what did all the rest matter? What did anything matter?

He, at any rate, could not live without her. He was not threatening her. He would not do anything melodramatic, but he would simply cease to live. It would not be necessary for him to do anything. Nature would do it for him. It would just be impossible for him to go on living.

He would be at Bertrand's studio that afternoon at three. Bertrand would not be there. Would she come and leave the answer there for him? He begged her to come, whateverthe answer was to be, even if it was to say goodbye to himfor ever.

Zita read the letter through twice. Jean's words lit up her face. She sat down and wrote a letter. This is what she wrote.

'You have guessed right. It is true. I will do what you ask me to do. I have thought about it and made up my mind. It is perhaps selfish what I am doing, perhaps bad for you. I love you too much to say "No". I will have no deception of Robert. Robert and I are by way of leaving for London tomorrow week. It is all settled beforehand, as is always his habit. The night before that I will start with you for Algiers. All I ask you to do is to send me a telegram with the name of the station and the hour the train starts. I will be there and I shall leave a letter for Robert telling him, but till then I will neither see you nor read any letters from you. Please do not try to meet me in anyone else's house.'

She took this letter to the studio and left it there. That same evening she received a telegram telling her the name of the station and the hour at which the train started for the south.

# CHAPTER VII

The afternoon following the day of Robert's departure Zita had tea with Amelia, and after they had been talking of various things, she said:

"I have got a piece of news for you, but you may have heard it already. Robert is going back to England for good."

She said this in a colourless, matter-of-fact way, as if it did not concern her. Amelia had not heard it. She had not been to the Bertrands, and Madeleine Laurent had left Paris for St Germain, where she was spending a few days. Amelia asked when they were going, and Zita told her all she knew. Amelia remembered afterwards that Zita had spoken throughout of Robert, and never of herself. Zita left. Amelia was bewildered. As soon as her husband came back that evening she talked it over with him.

"I can't understand Zita," she said. "I should have thought she would be miserable at the idea of leaving Paris just now that she has made friends and is having such fun, and going back to Wallington, of all places."

"Will they go there?"

"Zita will, unless Robert takes a house in London, which is unlikely. But instead of being miserable she seemed to me not only indifferent, but to be stifling excitement like a child that has been told it is going to be taken to the play."

"Will Jean mind?" said Cyril.

"No," said Amelia, "that is all over. But, do you think," she asked after a while, "that Robert could possibly have been jealous, a little green-eyed?"

"I think Robert is a *shrewd* man," said Cyril.

"Yes, one can't take him in, he can see through a brick wall, but I don't imagine Zita trying to, do you?"

"Then you think she never was in love with Jean?"

"No, never. I did think so for a moment; I was sure aboutit; but I think I was wrong, at least, I suppose I was wrong. Madeleine is sure she never cared for him. I think Jean got tired – Madeleine thinks Zita is an icicle, and I don't know whether she isn't right. I don't know what to think."

"I wonder why she married Robert?"

"Oh, that is simple," said Amelia, "it was the result of a first love affair that went wrong, and the wish not to disappoint her mother as her sisters had done, and to get away from pensions and hotels. And then I daresay she liked him. I think she does still like him."

"They never seem to me to speak to each other," said Cyril. "I often wonder what on earth they talk about."

"I forgot to tell you – the other night when we dined there and you and Flora were singing after dinner, what do you think Robert was reading …?"

"What?"

"Jean de Bosis' poems?"

Cyril laughed.

"He understands French," said Amelia, "although he says he doesn't, and I believe when we are not there he speaks it."

"I am sure he wouldn't understand those poems," said Cyril.

"I suppose not," said Amelia, "although he's fond of nature; and the poems are about ploughed fields."

"I believe," said Cyril, "he puts Zita on such a pedestal that he simply couldn't imagine her giving a thought to anyone in the world."

"Whatever he thinks, he's probably certain to be wrong, because men always are wrong."

"Are they, darling? I'm sure you know," said Cyril, laughing.

"We must have a farewell dinner for them," said Amelia, "and ask Jean."

"Of course; Jean and the Bertrands."

Robert came back from England. Everything, he said, had been arranged. Wallington would be ready for them in September. The lease on which the present tenant held it came to an end then, and Robert would not extend it.

The Harmers were to start on a Wednesday, and on the Sunday morning Zita went to Mass at Saint Philippe du Roule. Zita was not, or had not been until now, a religious woman. She was just *pratiquante*: that is to say, she went to Mass on Sundays and abstained on Fridays. She fulfilled her Easter duties. But that was all.

The church was crowded and stuffy. Zita was a prey to distractions till a Dominican got into the pulpit and began to preach. She found it was impossible not to listen to him, although she tried. He was eloquent and forcible, and he seemed to be speaking to her personally and individually, as if he was aware of her private difficulties and secret thoughts. He pointed out among other things how necessary it was that the individual should cheerfully accept sacrifice for the good of the community. The Church might seem hard on the individual; the hardness must be faced and accepted. He had spoken, too, of the stern necessity of duty, of the danger of illicit love. Zita listened to this eloquence unmoved. His words applied to her. They might have been directed at her personally and individually, but they did not affect her. She was determined to leave Robert; determined to go away with Jean. It was not that she was overwhelmingly swept away by passion for Jean; she could not say that. She was not really sure she loved him. But she was going. She said to herself that the eloquence of the Dominican's words had no effect on her whatsoever.

The Legges' farewell dinner came off that evening. They had asked the Bertrands, Madeleine Laurent, Mrs Rylands, one of the secretaries from the Embassy and his wife. Jean de Bosis was asked, but excused himself.

The guests could not take their eyes off Zita, as if they had been seeing her for the first time. She was dressed in black lace. On Amelia she made exactly the same impression as she had made when she had first told her Robert was going home. She was still like a child suffering from suppressed excitement, and so afraid of losing the coming treat that it does not dare even mention it.

Robert, on the other hand, seemed in rather forced good spirits; he was not like a schoolboy going home for the holidays, but like a schoolboy going back to school and pretending to like it.

When the guests were gone Amelia said to her husband:

"Well, how do you think it went off?"

"Robert doesn't seem so pleased at going as I should have expected," said Legge.

"He will miss Mrs Rylands," said Amelia.

"She told me she was going to London soon."

"How lovely Zita looked!"

"It's extraordinary. She oughtn't to be lovely on paper. Mrs Rylands said it was a pity she didn't dress better."

Amelia laughed. "She knows what suits her. She is independent of fashion. She looks like a princess in disguise."

"It's her expression that's half the battle," said Cyril.

"Oh, it's everything about her," said Amelia; "the men's faces were a study at dinner."

"And Robert seemed to be so proud of her."

"Oh yes, he is."

"I wonder what she feels?"

"What about?" he asked.

"About everything."

"I doubt if we shall ever know that."

"Well, you've known her for how many years? Four. Don't you feel you know her?"

"Not a bit better than the first day I set eyes on her."

When the Harmers got back to their flat that night the appearance of the apartment was depressing. The pictures were off the walls; the room was full of packed and half-packed packing-cases and trunks; the table strewn with old papers and old music, magazines, newspapers and every kind of junk. Near a half-packed box, Robert's Airedale terrier, Tinker, was keeping a sullen watch. The door of the sitting-room opening into Robert's study was open, and Robert's study, Zita noticed, was bare. A waste-paper basket was near the writing-table overflowing with papers and photographs he had destroyed: among these she noticed at once a photograph of a group which had been taken of him and herself and her mother when they were engaged, at Nice. It had always been on his writing-table wherever they had been. It had been taken the day they were engaged. Robert had always been particularly fond of this photograph.

She was on the verge of saying, "They've thrown away the Nice group," but she reflected he must have done it himself. Why?

Robert read a letter which he found waiting for him, and then said to Zita:

"I shall have to start tomorrow."

"Oh!" she said. "Tomorrow morning?"

"Yes; tomorrow morning."

It was on Tuesday evening that she was to meet Jean at the station. Zita had not changed her mind.

"But there's no reason why you should come," he went on, "you won't have time to pack; and you had better stay on a few more days," he said. "You could stay on another week if you like, and I can come back and fetch you. That will be the best arrangement. I have sublet the apartment, but it is ours till the end of the month, and Amélie and Joseph can stay on another week."

Zita said nothing.

"You can think it over and settle tomorrow," said Robert. "But I'm sure you won't want to hurry."

At that moment the dog, Tinker, came and put his paws on her lap and looked her in the face in an appealing manner, as if to say, "Don't go away." The dog was fond of her, and she loved him.

"Tinker knows," she said to herself.

"Tinker will miss you," said Robert, and as he looked at her his eyes seemed to see right through her. Zita could say nothing. "He must come with me tomorrow," he added, as if explaining the remark and making it natural. "Did you write and thank Jean de Bosis," Robert said, "for sending you his book?"

"No," she said truthfully.

"Well, you had better write to him tomorrow; he is going away: to Algiers."

Zita was startled.

"I know because Williamson heard him order his tickets at Cook's." Robert stressed the plural. "He ordered," he went on, "two sleeping-compartments with a place for his servant. So he is not going alone. He is taking either his mother…"

"Or?" repeated Zita mechanically.

"Or his mistress."

At that moment Zita, who was not, as a rule, a perceptive woman, knew, and knew for certain, that Robert knew. Knew that she meant to leave him; to go away with Jean de Bosis. How, she had no idea; but she had absolute faith in this sudden fit of lucidity. He not only knew, but he was making it easy for her; helping her; making it unnecessary for her to lie to him, or enabling her to lie as little as possible. She still felt no twinge of remorse, and no prick of conscience, but now, when Robert stood there in front of her looking at her with his far-seeing honest eyes, when he said the word 'mistress', revealing to her what she took to be his certain knowledge, the categoric imperative swept by her like a spirit. She knew she could not go away.

"I shan't want any more time for packing," she said. "I shall be quite ready to come with you tomorrow. All my things are packed." This was true.

"Good night, Robert."

"Good night," said Robert, lighting a cigar. "You must think over it, and don't forget to write to Jean de Bosis."

# CHAPTER VIII

Zita left Paris the next morning with Robert Harmer, and before starting she wrote two letters; one to Jean and one to Amelia Legge. To Amelia she said that they had been obliged to start a day earlier than they had expected, and she begged her to make her excuses where it was necessary.

To Jean she wrote that she had found at the last moment she could not leave her husband; she had not changed, and did not think she would change, but she knew she would only make him, Jean, unhappy if she left Robert.

A few days later Amelia Legge heard from Zita, who said that she had arrived safely in London. About a fortnight later still Madeleine burst in on Amelia one morning and said she had things of importance to tell her. Jean was ill. At one moment his life had been despaired of. His mother was nursing him in his apartment. She, Madeleine Laurent, had been away during the last fortnight at Fontainebleau, and had only just heard the news. Madame de Bosis had been to see her. It had been brain fever, apparently. Now he was out of danger.

"Was it because of Zita?" Amelia asked.

"His mother says so," said Madeleine. "He seems to have been stunned by her departure, then demented, then ill."

"But how extraordinary!" said Amelia, "he had stopped

going near her."

"He had probably given it up as hopeless, but that did not prevent him feeling what he felt. Madame de Bosis says he was in love with Zita, and that she led him on and then left him.She is furious with her, of course. And she says that is how all Englishwomen behave, that she is a cold-hearted flirt: cold-hearted and hot-blooded. We had a long discussion, and I tried to make her admit that Zita's going away was the best thing that could have happened. But all she said was: 'You don't know Jean. He's not like the others. He will never get over it.' I said they would have been equally unhappy whatever else had happened. Suppose she had run away with Jean, I said. 'God forbid,' Madame de Bosis had answered. 'Well, then, what?' I asked, 'an ordinary liaison?'… 'Whatever they did, the mischief was done,' she said. 'My son has been poisoned by that woman.'"

"And what do you think, Madeleine?" asked Amelia.

"I think," said Madeleine, "that she did not love him and that she never did love him. I think Jean loved her and saw it was hopeless. That he left off seeing her, thought he was cured, and found when she went away that he was not cured at all. Of course, I do not pretend to understand *vous autres*."

"But it is just as difficult for me," said Amelia plaintively. "I don't pretend to understand Zita; and the more I see of her, and the longer I know her, the less I feel I understand her."

"And Harmer?" asked Madeleine, "did he perhaps play a part?"

"I wonder," said Amelia, "Robert is by no means a fool."

"If he was jealous it might explain everything," said Madeleine.

"He couldn't have been jealous of Jean," said Amelia, "Zita has not set eyes on him for weeks."

"That is of no consequence," said Madeleine, "it is not what people do that make men jealous, but what they are. It is the instinct of the male that leads men to be jealous of the right person. That is why it's not the cleverest men who are the least easily deceived, but often quite ordinary men who have the male instinct. I imagine Mr Harmer had it."

"Quite possibly," said Amelia, "but there was nothing to have it about."

"Who knows?"

"Oh! if it comes to that, we know nothing! Did Jean tell his mother anything?"

"Not a word, and in his delirium he raved the whole time about someone called Marie."

"Well, you see! Zita was never called Marie."

"It was fatal for Jean to meet your Zita," said Madeleine. "She was fated by her beauty, her peculiar beauty, which would not be admired by everyone, still less by every Frenchman, to inspire a passion in a man like Jean, and she was equally destined by her nature and her circumstances to be incapable of satisfying it. It is a great pity."

"Perhaps it is just as well for both their sakes," said Amelia. "Why shouldn't Jean marry someone and be happy?"

"Because he is one of those people who are not born for happiness."

"Poor boy!" said Amelia, with a tearful voice, "I should like him to be happy," (and then petulantly) "He ought to be happy."

Jean recovered slowly. He told his mother nothing. He left Paris and retired to her house in Normandy, where he started to write a novel.

The Legges saw nothing of him, neither did the Bertrands.

Amelia Legge heard from Zita from time to time. Robert had taken a house at Wimbledon, where they were to live until the tenant who had taken Wallington left. But when the time came for him to leave, the tenant proposed renewing the lease for five years, and Robert consented. The truth was that while nothing would persuade Robert to take a house in London, Zita had suddenly made it clear to him that nothing would persuade her to live at Wallington. She had her mother, who was in England, to back her up. She told Mrs Mostyn that sooner than live at Wallington she would leave Robert for good, and Mrs Mostyn persuaded Robert that she meant this. Robert did not greatly care if he lived at Wallington or not so long as he did not live in London. Living at Wimbledon enabled him to drive up to London every day. He resolved to take a shooting-lodge in Scotland every autumn. He easily could go racing from Wimbledon, and he could always sleep at the club when he wanted to; moreover, Mrs Rylands had taken a house in London for three years, so everyone was satisfied.

A new life began for Zita. After her brief hour not of fame, but of notice, for she had not only been admired by the French in Paris, but her beauty had been a topic of discussion among English visitors, she passed once more into obscurity and permanent eclipse. She lived as one in a dream. She saw few people; she hardly ever went out in London, except every now and then to some small dinner party or perhaps to a musical evening given by one of Robert's city friends. She seemed not to care; to be neither happy nor unhappy; just listless, like a person who had been drugged. It was the truth. She had been numbed by what had happened, and was like a person who has taken a narcotic.

Robert was attentive and devoted to her as before, and did everything he could to please her, but all his efforts were of no avail. Nothing he did seemed to rouse her. She walked amiable and beautiful through life like someone in a trance.

She seemed to have no interests. She had no real friends, and few acquaintances. Her mother died soon after they came back to England; her sisters both continued to live abroad.

She was not a reader; when she had first married she read every novel that came her way, and now, as if suffering from all that surfeit, she never opened a book. She was not wrapped up in her religion; she fulfilled her duties and no more. She knew no priests. But she had one engrossing hobby, and that filled her life. It was perhaps more than enough. It was her garden. She had suffered at Wallington from not being able to create a garden. There was one already, a large one; large, but irremediable, and under the eye and relentless hand of a competent North countryman who was not going to change anything: so Zita did not even enter the lists with him. But when she came to live at Wimbledon there was a large garden and a tame gardener, and she set about to create a garden such as she wanted, and Robert was delighted that she should have an occupation. It filled her life, and the garden which she created was, if people could have seen it, one of the sights of England.

It was a masterpiece of taste and design, a riot of cunningly devised and arranged colour. A feast to the eye, a rest to the body; the shade and the light were in the right place. As it was, few people saw it except Robert's business friends. And all they said was "Quite a nice lot of flowers you've got, Robert. I suppose *you* do all that, you always were a clever gardener. Those chrysanthemums are doing well," pointing to the bergamots.

It is a surprising, but not an uncommon, thing that a woman as beautiful as Zita (and as time went on she became more rather than less beautiful – she was twice as beautiful now as she had been when she had first come out), should, after having been recognized as a beauty in Paris by the French and the English, have lived for nearly ten years in the suburbs of London, now and then paying visits in the counties of England, without attracting more attention than she did. She was the reverse of a professional beauty. She had been forgotten and was never rediscovered.

There is not one single portrait extant of her by an English artist. The only two pictures that exist of her are the two that Bertrand painted: one of which is at Wallington and the other at the Luxembourg in Paris. She was photographed once or twice on a seaside pier or at a fair, but never by a photographer of note. She went to no large entertainments and took part in no public functions. She was unknown to the general public and unnoticed by any public. She lived alone, content, apparently, in her garden, and looked after her husband.

He seemed to be happy. Zita fitted in with his ideas of comfort. He liked ordering dinner, but he liked someone to see that his orders were carried out in the way he liked. That is just what Zita did. She did more: much more. She appeared to do nothing, but she did everything: she always had, and Amelia and others had been deceived and wrong about her.

Robert was happy in his business. He did well. He got richer and richer. Every year he spent one month in Scotland in the shooting-lodge he took, and later in the autumn he would stay for a week with friends for the pheasant-shooting. He attended the Derby regularly, also the Grand National, the St Leger, and at least one autumn and one spring meeting at Newmarket. He entertained his city friends at Wimbledon. The cooking was good and the wines excellent. In addition to everything else, he saw Mrs Rylands every day. She now lived permanently in London, originally to look after a niece, but, now that the niece was married, because she had become so fond of England that she would feel a stranger or an exile were she to go back to Paris, and still more so were she to go back to America.

What were their relations? Nobody ever knew. Mrs Rylands was a handsome woman about the same age as Robert, possibly younger than he was and looking older than her age, or possibly older than he was and looking younger than her age. She was large, smooth and blonde, with a short Greek nose and magnificent shoulders and rather lustreless eyes, one of those women who are born handsome. She was sensible and universally liked. Whatever their other relations might be, Robert venerated her opinions on every subject in the world, and believed in her absolutely.

She, in this delicate situation, behaved with tact and did all she could not to annoy Zita or interfere with her. Mrs Rylands disliked women as a rule, but she did not mind Zita. Secretly, in her heart of hearts, she probably thought it was a great shame that Robert Harmer had married such a wife. He ought to have married a woman of the world with a great deal of character who would have pushed him on and helped him and been a real companion, whereas Zita was hopeless, mooning about in a suburban garden and not knowing a soul... She may have thought such thoughts, but if she did she did not express them. She never made things difficult for Zita; she was far too naturally shrewd.

Zita, on the other hand, seemed to be delighted that Robert should be friends with her, and accepted her as a matter of course. The unwritten rules of the game were observed on both sides with the greatest punctilio. Robert stayed two nights a week in London for dinner – it was called dining at the club. Once a month Robert and Zita gave a small dinner party, to which Mrs Rylands was invited. She never dined by herself at 'The Birches', the name of Robert's house, but she sometimes, though rarely, had tea with Zita when Robert was not there.

Sometimes she gave a dinner party, to which Zita and Robert were both invited. It was small, and meant going to the play. They drove home in a brougham. Zita accepted one of these invitations once a year and declined the others, and Robert went by himself.

Robert took Mrs Rylands to the races with a party of other friends, and she always stayed in Scotland at the Lodge.

During the next few years Zita never went abroad, except one Easter, when they spent a week in Florence and a week in Rome. Robert Harmer went often to Paris on business, and for the Grand Prix and other meetings, and once to Monte Carlo. He suggested that Zita should accompany him, but she declined. They heard little from or of their Paris friends.

The Legges had been appointed to Tokyo soon after the Harmers left Paris, and they stayed there four years, at the end of which time they went to Stockholm.

The year after the Harmers left Paris, Jean de Bosis

published a book, which made him famous. It was inprose this time, and startlingly different in tone and subject from his volume of verse. It was a short novel dealing with contemporary life: bitter, cynical, rather crude, extremely vivid; and it surprised, shocked, and captivated the public. In the Press it was praised by some and attacked by many. It was discussed by everyone; translated into many languages, but not into English. Jean de Bosis did not send Zita a copy of the book, and she never read it, although echoes of its notoriety reached her through Mrs Rylands, who said "it was disagreeable, although, of course, very well written".

A year later Jean published a second book. Fantastic this time and full of colour and sensuality, and some people said the crudest coarseness. This book had a definite success of scandal, and was banned by libraries or booksellers in some countries. Jean came in for a torrent of abuse in France, and he excited the anger of the best and serenest critics, who burst into a chorus of frenzied vituperation; they all agreed that this time he had gone too far. But his sales grew larger than ever. His book was dramatised, turned, that is to say, into a long and crude melodrama. This was extremely successful, too. Then, as if in defiance of criticism, Jean set about to exaggerate the faults which the critics had complained of. His next book read like an imitation of his own manner in which the faults were exaggerated and the mannerisms caricatured. This often happens with writers whose work at the same time excites the vituperation of the critics and wins the favour of the public – the author tends as a result to abound in himself. Not two hours after writing these lines I came across in a book just published a passage referring to Bulwer Lytton, in which the author[1] said that a "combination of readers' enthusiasm and critics' brutality always worked on Bulwer's peculiar

1. M. Sadleir

temperament in such a way as to bring out the worst of his many mannerisms". This sentence exactly fits Jean de Bosis, and might have been written about him.

The new book was more successful than ever with the public. The critics had little left to say. They had already used all their powder and shot. They contented themselves by saying that Jean de Bosis was "finished" and written out.

After that he produced a new book every year: "the same book," his enemies said, "slightly deteriorating year by year."

The year his second book appeared he married a singer. Her name was Emilia Altenbrandt. She was the widow of an Austrian. Her own nationality was mixed. "She might have been a Russian, French, or Turk, or Prussian, or perhaps Italian," but what she exactly 'remained', it was difficult to say: not French certainly, and not English. She spoke most languages and could be silent in none. She was handsome, dark, and flamboyant, exhausting and exacting. She sang *Lieder* in French, German and Italian, and sometimes in Russian, all over the Continent. She was more than successful among the musical publics of Europe. They went mad over her, but she had not been to England. It was not for want of being asked by the concert managers, but she refused to come; the climate, she said, would kill her, and she was a woman who knew her own mind.

Mrs Rylands told Zita all about her and her marriage, all about Jean's success and Emilia Altenbrandt's success, of the triumphs they were both enjoying all over Europe: at Vienna, St Petersburg, Berlin, Rome, Milan, Madrid; of their great happiness, and of the wild ecstasy of their double worldwide fame.

Zita listened with calm as to a story that happened a long time ago.

"A great while since, a long, long time ago."

# CHAPTER IX

It was not until nine years after they had left Paris, the year of the next great Paris Exhibition – that of the Eiffel Tower – that Zita Harmer for a second time came in contact and in touch with her old Paris friends.

Robert was ordered by his doctor to take the waters at Haréville, and he obeyed his doctor's orders. They went there in the middle of July.

Robert took the waters. Zita merely looked on. The first person she met the morning after her arrival, as she strolled through the Galéries looking at the shop windows, was Amelia Legge, not much changed; a little bit greyer, perhaps, and perhaps even more voluble and plaintive than before. She told Zita all her news in the first five minutes of their meeting. Cyril was now Councillor at Paris; he was arriving the next day, or as soon as he could; he had not to drink the waters. She had to drink the lighter, not the stronger, waters for her eyes. They were back again in Paris, but not, alas, at their old apartment; they had taken one on the other side of the river.

"It's wonderful to see you again, Zita," said Amelia, "and looking not a day older; on the contrary, more beautiful than ever. Madeleine Laurent is alive and flourishing, and Jean de Bosis is married and famous, even more famous than his wife. We never met her, but we heard her at Berlin. He writes too much...and it is a great pity. I found his last book fearfully interesting, in fact, I think all his books are interesting. Cyril says I am wrong, and, of course, I know they shock a great many people. They are shocking, there's no denying it, but they don't shock *me*, so few books do," she said, with an apologetic sigh.

"I haven't read any of them," said Zita. "I never seem to have time to read now; I'm always busy."

"Busy at what?"

"Oh, lots of things – gardening chiefly."

"Ah, you've got a garden now, at Wimbledon. You don't live at Wallington?"

"Wallington is still let."

"I think that is sensible of Robert. Wallington wasn't a possible place to live in, it was too dark, bleak, too cold, too large, and too uncomfortable."

"I sometimes wonder whether Robert doesn't miss it."

"Oh! nonsense, Zita; don't think such things. If he missed it he would live there. Men, you know, don't do what they don't want to. Here is Robert," she said, as Robert strode towards them in white flannels and a straw hat. He looked, Amelia thought, considerably older and rather ill. No wonder he was taking the waters. He looked infirm, grey and thin, and slightly care-worn. He greeted his cousin warmly.

That was the first of many meetings, and the more Amelia saw of her cousin and her cousin-in-law, the more she wondered, and the more she wondered the more impossible she found it to come to any conclusion.

Mrs Rylands was not at Haréville, but after the Harmers had been there for some days it turned out that the doctor at the watering-place where she was staying, which was ten miles off – a long distance in those days – told her that the waters were not strong enough for her, and that she had better try those of Haréville, which he was sure would suit her better. She obeyed her doctor, and almost at the same time Cyril Legge arrived from Paris, and with him Jean de Bosis, without his wife. Jean de Bosis had been ordered a course of the waters, but his wife said she could not endure the monotony and the dullness of Haréville, and he was to meet her at Venice, where they had taken the first floor of a palace, for later on, as soon as he should have finished his cure.

Jean de Bosis met and talked with the Harmers with the utmost ease and friendliness. Zita thought he was altered; Amelia thought not. It was not that he looked much older – he was thirty-nine and looked younger – but his expression was, Zita thought, different. It had hardened. She wondered what had happened to him, and what he felt. He was a new man to her, as if she had never known him. But to Jean de Bosis, Zita seemed no different. There was no doubt about that. She seemed to him just as beautiful, perhaps more beautiful than she had been ten years ago. Amelia noticed this, and commented on it.

"He admires you just as much as ever," she said one morning to Zita, while they were sitting in the park listening to the band.

"Oh! I don't think so," said Zita.

"It is perfectly obvious, and if you're not careful he'll be in love with you. I used to think he was in love, or going to be in love, with you in Paris in old days."

Zita laughed.

"Did you think that?"

"Yes, I did. I think he *was* at one time, for a moment, only you were so…well, I suppose you didn't care for him and gave him no encouragement."

"His wife is beautiful, isn't she?"

"Not exactly beautiful, but handsome. And a remarkable woman, and her singing is wonderful. You've never heard her?"

"No, she's never been to England. Is he very fond of her?"

"He certainly was at first, they say, but I think they both have bad tempers. She's obviously the woman he described in his book, well, in all his books, but chiefly in *Le Philtre*."

"I must read it. He isn't musical, is he?" asked Zita.

"Oh no! He hates music, and she hates literature. That was one reason, I suppose, they were attracted to one another."

"Is she much younger than he is?"

"No, older, she was a widow when she married him."

"And are there no children?"

"There was one; it died."

But soon Zita was able to get firsthand impressions of Jean de Bosis. Robert got up early in the morning, and drank his first glass of water at half past six. Owing to this he felt tired in the afternoon, and he took a long siesta. Jean did not begin his cure until much later, and it was of a much milder nature. The day after his arrival, at two o'clock in the afternoon, he found Zita sitting by herself under the shade of a tree in the park. She always sat in the same chair under the same tree doing needlework. The Legges had gone out driving, so Jean took a chair and sat down next to Zita. It was the first time in his life he had been able to talk to her completely by himself, that is to say without the presence of witnesses or of observant friends, who, although they might not be listening, were there.

"Why did you do it?" were his first words.

"Do what?"

"Say you would come with me and not come?"

"Robert knew," she said.

"What did he do?"

"He did nothing, and said nothing; that was just it."

"How did he know?"

"I don't know, but he knew, and he was making things easy for me. He was helping me out; helping me not to lie; it was terrible."

"Did he read my book?"

"Which book?"

"The book of poems I sent you."

67

"Yes, he did, some of it, with some trouble."

"Then of course he knew."

"Why?"

"Because there was a poem about you in it."

"Robert would never have thought that. He liked something about wild ducks; but that would never have occurred to him; that poem might have been about anyone. It never occurred to anyone that it was meant for me – nor to Amelia or Madeleine Laurent – they would have told me at once."

"It would not have occurred to them, but it would to your husband. There are some things that only men understand; just as there are some things that only women understand. That is one of them – one of men's things."

"But Robert doesn't know what poetry is about."

"He knew what that poem was about – that one and the one about the wild ducks."

"You think so?"

"I know. You know I was ill."

"When I went away?"

"Yes, when you went away. So ill – I nearly died. You knew what my illness was?"

"Yes, I knew. I could do nothing. I could have run away with you, and I couldn't do that, so I could do nothing."

There was a long pause.

"But now are you happy?" Zita asked, not looking at him.

"Happy?" he said, with a slightly harsh laugh.

"At any rate, you are famous."

"Oh yes." His laughter was harsher and more bitter. "That's just it."

"You are not pleased with your books? I have not read one of them."

"Thank God! But it's your fault."

"What?"

"That my books are what they are. If you had come with me they would have been different; they would have been like my first book; like what I wrote for you. Perhaps you saved your soul, but you lost mine."

"Don't say that. Whatever I did wrong I have paid for, I assure you. After all, life is like that. Who is happy?"

"You may well ask. I believe my wife is. She is happy in her art, in her success, and, most of all, in the society of the band of *cabotins* who surround her wherever she goes."

"I believe," said Zita, "that work is the secret of happiness. I have got no work, but I have an occupation; I have made a garden."

"How lovely it must be," said Jean, with dreamy eyes.

They talked of the Bertrands; they talked of Madeleine Laurent; they talked of the Legges; of Jean's travels, and as they talked the time rushed by. The band in the kiosk began to play a selection from *La Mascotte*, and Zita got up abruptly and said she must fetch her husband; it was time for her to wake him.

That night they all dined together at the same table. Robert was friendly with Jean. The next day exactly the same thing happened. The routine continued to be the same every day. Robert took his long siesta and the Legges went for a drive, because Amelia liked sketching. Zita sat in her chair. Jean joined her. They talked of everything under the sun, easily and without sense of effort or of time. Like Krylov's two pigeons, they never heeded how the time flew by. Sadness they knew; they were never anything but sad, but they never tasted the weariness of satiety – what Shelley calls 'love's sad satiety'.

For Jean did not make love to Zita. They seemed to be living in a dream. They lived, as it were, in the past, and not in the present. Every night they sat at the same table. A fortnight passed like this before they noticed it. Robert's cure was to last three weeks.

There is a fragment of a Greek poem which tells of the pause that occurs midmost in the winter month, when, the poet says, Zeus brings fourteen days of calm, and mortals call it the sacred windless breeding time of the many-coloured halcyon.

So in the lives of Zita and Jean came a brief interval of halcyon days.

Never had life seemed more peaceful and uneventful to Zita, Robert and Jean; and yet never had fate been more busy weaving the irreparable for all three of them.

It was at the end of their fortnight that Amelia said at dinner that she had written to Madeleine and told her all the news. Madeleine was at the time at Versailles – and going backwards and forwards between Versailles and Paris. She had told her in her letter, among other things, that Jean de Bosis was at Haréville, and seemed to admire Zita more than ever. The day Madeleine received this letter she met Madame Jean de Bosis at a *déjeuner*. She talked of Jean, said she knew that he was at Haréville, and added, "He will have met some old friends – an Englishman and his wife whom he used to know ten years ago in Paris."

"Oh," said Madame de Bosis, "that will be nice for him." She was not interested.

"Yes," said Madeleine, slightly nettled at her want of interest. "Harmer and Mrs Harmer. She is beautiful – Bertrand painted her twice."

That was enough for Emilia de Bosis. She left for Haréville the next day. She arrived in the evening. She had announced her arrival by a telegram, and she made no objection when her husband told her that they would dine at the same table with the Legges and the Harmers – that is to say, with the Leggesand Mrs Harmer, because those who drank stronger waters –Mr Harmer and Mrs Rylands – dined at the table d'hôte at six, where a special diet was served them.

Emilia explained her arrival by saying that her husband's presence at Haréville had been noised abroad, and she had been asked to sing for charity at the concert which was to take place at Haréville on the following Sunday. On Monday, she said, she and Jean were going to Venice. Jean had told Zita he was staying another week, as long, in fact, as she and Robert were staying; but that was all changed now.

Emilia de Bosis made herself the centre of the group, as she was in the habit of doing in any group anywhere. She ate heartily; she drank sparingly; she talked a great deal; she sometimes smiled, but she never laughed. When dinner was over and they were drinking coffee outside, she said they must all go to the theatre; she wished, she said, to feel the atmosphere of the house, as she was to sing in it on Sunday. Zita and the Legges consented, but Mrs Rylands and Robert said they would go to the Casino.

At the table next to them sat a young man by himself, who watched their whole party with absorbed interest. He was a journalist, Walter Price by name, a British subject, although he had lived and worked for some years in America, and still wrote for American newspapers as well as for an English one. He was strikingly good-looking; big, well-made, and hard to place at first sight. He did not look like an Englishman, but neither did he look particularly like anything else; his face was square, with straight features and a low forehead, and he reminded Zita, who noticed him directly, of a bust, Classic or Renaissance, she had seen somewhere, either one of the Roman emperors or an Italian *Condottiere*, she thought.

Just as the Harmers and their friends were leaving the little table where they had drunk coffee outside on the veranda and were preparing to go into the Casino, Price, who had a great deal of quiet assurance, and did not know what shyness meant, walked up to Jean and talked to him. Jean did not for the moment recall him or place him…as I have said, he was hard to place…but in a moment he recollected having met him several times at first nights, or on other artistic or maybe sporting occasions in Paris.

"I want Madame to give me an interview for the *Planet*," he began.

"I don't think she …" Jean said, so as to be on the safe side, but his wife overheard the conversation, and interrupted him:

"Good evening, Mr Price," she said, giving him her hand. "We are old friends," she explained to Jean. "Come to my salon tomorrow at eleven. I have things I want to ask you about this concert."

Price was delighted; all the more so because Madame de Bosis, although he had twice been presented to her before, had never recognised him when they had met on subsequent occasions; but this wasn't what he wanted now. He wanted to be introduced to Mrs Harmer, and as they walked towards the theatre he asked Jean to introduce him.

"With pleasure," Jean said, and he introduced Walter Price to the Legges and to Zita.

# CHAPTER X

The concert came off on Sunday night, but Emilia de Bosis did not sing at it because she received, so she said, an urgent summons to go to Venice at once from an impresario who had come all the way from Vienna to meet her. Jean and she left the morning after her arrival, and Jean had no conversation alone with Zita from the moment his wife arrived.

The Harmers and the Legges and Mrs Rylands stayed on another week. Walter Price stayed, too, and he saw a great deal of them. By degrees he attached himself to them, and ended before the week was over by becoming an integral part of their little group.

At the end of the week the Harmers went to Gérardmer on the advice of Robert's doctor, who wished him to have an after-cure. The Legges went with them, and Walter Price. Mrs Rylands said she felt as comfortable with Walter Price as she did with a real American. Robert Harmer said he thought he was not a bad fellow, but it was a pity he spoke with an American accent. Cyril Legge said it was catching. Amelia liked him, and so did Zita. She got on with him without any trouble. She felt as if she had always known him. They went together on the lake: they all went together for expeditions near and far. They spent an enjoyable week, at the end of which the Harmers and Mrs Rylands went back to England and the others to Paris.

Walter Price announced his intention of visiting London later on. He came to England in the winter. The Harmers followed their regular routine; in August they had spent a month in Scotland shooting with Wilfrid Sutton and his wife, and one or two others as guests; later on they paid a few visits in the north of England, and by November they settled down once more at Wimbledon.

Walter Price came to London soon after this. He hadgot himself permanently transferred to London, and he was making a name for himself in journalism as a writer of clever impressionistic articles and interviews – he was an all-round journalist, and seemed to be able to turn his hand to anything: sport, the stage, books, nature, social events, political meetings, occasions and personages; he was smart and superficial as a writer, and unhampered by distinction or refinement. He came to Wimbledon as often as he could, but that was not often, as he was a hard-worked man, and his work took him all over the country; one day he would be attendinga football match in the north of England and the next at a political meeting in South Devon, or interviewing someone in Dublin or Glasgow. Notwithstanding the comparative rarity of his visits, he came to know Zita well. He admired her, looked up to her, and was happy in her society. He poured out toher haphazard and without choice or discrimination his adventures, thoughts, troubles, joys, cares, hopes, ambitions… everything, in fact. He talked exclusively about himself, and she liked it. Never had she felt so much at her ease, so comfortable with any human being. So matters went on until the spring, when Walter Price was sent by his newspaper to America. He was away the whole summer, and Zita missed him, seldom as she had seen him while he had been in England. Without knowing it she had become used to him, and he had brought something into her life that hitherto had been absent, something she had never known before – namely, companionship and gaiety: because Walter was gay; he had an un-English buoyancy and quickness he had caught in America; he was appreciative, and had an infectious laugh, and he thought Zita funny, and roared with laughter at some of her remarks. This was the first time anything of this kind had happened to her.

When July came again, Robert Harmer was advised by his doctors to repeat his cure at Haréville. He arranged to go there at the same time as the Legges. The day before the Harmers were to start, Walter Price came back from America and went straight down to Wimbledon. When he heard their plans he told them by an odd coincidence he had also been ordered to Haréville. His decision to go there was taken on the spur of the moment. He had on his arrival applied for and been granted three weeks holiday, but until he saw the Harmers he had no intention of going to Haréville.

Both the Harmers were delighted. Walter Price amused Robert.

Mrs Rylands was to join them in a few days. They would find the Legges at the hotel. All was the same as it had been last year, but Zita was aware that everything was different. Life to her was now a different thing, different from anything it had ever been. It was lined and shot with a curious excitement.She was anxious as she had never been before as soon as one day was over for the next day to begin.

It was when Walter arrived at Haréville that she first faced the situation, and said to herself: 'What has happened to me?' She thought of any answer except the true one, which she refused to give herself. 'I am forty; he is not thirty. I am almost old enough to be his mother...and yet there is no doubt that since he has come back from America life has been different; but quite different.' She knew she had, when she was with him, the feeling of timelessness; that she felt she could go on talking and listening to him for ever. She never wanted their intercourse to stop.

As for Walter Price, he seemed to enjoy it, too; but he never appeared to wish to be alone with Zita; he was just as happy if

Robert or the Legges were there, nor did he ever resent a tête-à-tête with Zita being interrupted. He seemed to be happy with all of them, as if he were a part of their family or group, something essential and integral which belonged to them and could not live without them.

He paid just as much attention to Mrs Legge, and to Mrs Rylands when she arrived, as he did to Zita.

One or two mornings after Zita had arrived at Haréville she was sitting in the park talking to Amelia Legge when Amelia said to her:

"Do you ever hear anything of Jean de Bosis?"

Zita said he had sometimes written to her, but she had heard nothing of or from him for some months.

"Well, I can tell you a little about him," said Amelia. "He's written another book, as you probably know, a fearfully interesting book, but rather shocking, only, as usual, it don't shock me! I suppose I'm hardened. And his wife has been singing all over the world, just as usual. They went to Russia in the winter. I saw them sometimes in Paris this spring, but not often. I don't think he's at all happy. He told me the last time I saw him some months ago that he would come here in the summer."

"Oh!" said Zita.

"Yes, and he asked after you."

Zita smiled. Jean de Bosis seemed to her to belong to something infinitely far away, both in space and in time.

"He's not happy," Amelia went on, "his wife's friends bore him and his friends bore her. They can't really live together and they can't do without one another."

"She's still fond of him?" asked Zita.

"Oh yes, and desperately jealous. She has never looked at anyone else. He would have if he dared, but he doesn't dare! She has a tremendous hold over him. She's a wonderful woman, in a way. She's not only a great artist – and she is, without doubt, a really great artist, and the best concert singer alive, I suppose, and that's a rare thing – but she is a remarkable woman as well, and that's rarer still."

"They never come to England," said Zita.

"No, she doesn't like England, or rather the thought of it, because she doesn't know it. He looks much older than he did. He is tired with all that writing, and all the wrangle of their domestic life, and all that travel."

"It must be very tiring," said Zita.

It was clear during all this conversation that she was only faintly interested in Jean de Bosis, but she was not entirely conscious of the fact. She was conscious of it two days later, when the manager of the hotel announced to her that Jean de Bosis was arriving.

"Is Madame de Bosis coming too?" she asked.

The manager said no; not at present, at any rate.

He arrived the next night by himself.

He went straight to Zita and asked if he might sit at her table. They dined together that night: Zita, the Legges, Jean de Bosis and Walter Price. Robert Harmer and Mrs Rylands had dined at the table d'hôte.

He said that he had been ordered to take the waters. His wife was at the Mont Dore for her throat. She was with a party of musical friends.

"They didn't want me," he said, "and I doubt whether I could have supported the Mont Dore and so many musicians for all that time. Anyhow, the matter was settled by the doctor, who said I was to come here."

He looked, indeed, as if he needed a cure somewhere; ten years older than he had looked the year before. After dinner they sat out in the garden until it was time to go to bed.

The next day in the early afternoon Jean de Bosis walked into the park, expecting to find Zita at the usual place in her chair. She was there, but Walter Price was there too. He did not go away when Jean de Bosis came, but stayed until Zita went to fetch her husband, and talked incessantly.

The evening was spent like the preceding one, except that they went to see a play in the Casino. Before they went to bed Jean managed to say to Zita:

"I must have a talk with you alone some time tomorrow. Let us go for a little walk in the park after *déjeuner*."

Zita nodded. She had no wish to go for a walk with Jean. She realized this, but she did not know how to refuse. It was at that moment that the truth began to break upon her, but not wholly. She knew that she did not want to see Jean de Bosis. She did not want to see anyone but Walter Price, and she wanted to see him every day and every moment of the day, but yet she did not put the question to herself: 'Am I in love with him?' She only knew that nothing like this had happened to her before. She slept badly that night. She did not know what to do about Jean.

'I suppose I must see him,' she said to herself, 'but what shall I say to him?'

And at the same time she wondered how she could still manage to see Walter. The matter was settled for her. M. Carnot, the President of the Republic, was passing through Nancy for some ceremony or inauguration, and Price's editor telegraphed to him to attend the ceremony, and if possible to obtain an interview with anyone of importance with regard to the relations of the Royalist and any other parties who had been intriguing with General Boulanger, now utterly discredited. Price had to catch a train early in the morning. There was no escape for Zita. Jean found her in her usual place just after *déjeuner*.

"I have been waiting for this moment the whole year," he said.

"Really?" said Zita. She wanted to appear as friendly as possible. "I am very glad to see you again." This phrase, with its all too-friendly accent, its accent of a friendliness, that is to say, that could only mean indifference, was like a knell to Jean.

"I see," he said, "it is all over."

"What?"

"All that used to be, and all that might have been."

"I did not know there *was* anything."

"You have forgotten last year?"

Zita felt she might well have said that it was surely he who had shown least signs of remembrance, since she had only heard from him once or twice since the past year, but she did not wish to seem to have a grievance. He voiced her thoughts.

"You think because I made so few signs of life that I had forgotten?" he said. "I have forgotten nothing. I could do nothing because of Emilia. She guessed at once, and was fearfully jealous. We had scenes and reconciliations, terrible scenes! and even more terrible reconciliations! over and over again. I once nearly killed her. I tried to kill myself. I know I was weak and despicable, and I do not deny she had real, complete power over me. She dominated me altogether, but now that is over…at least it might be over if you would help me. I could be free at last for the first time. She knows why I have come here. She knows the truth, that I hate her and thatI love you, and that I cannot live without you."

"Oh, don't – " said Zita frightened.

"Then it is all over?" said Jean, savagely, "and I know why – I knew why at once, directly I saw you, but I tried to deceive myself."

"What do you mean?"

"You are in love with that vulgar reporter, Price. But I warn you you're making a mistake; he's not a *real* person."

Zita blushed scarlet, and, like a blinding flash, the truth came to her fully for the first time. She knew that this was true; that she loved Walter; that she had loved him from the first, from the moment she had first set eyes on him. She had, when she had first seen Walter, been struck with fatal lightning, which is always the herald of a real passion and never of a passing fancy, but which, unfortunately, so rarely happens at the same time to both parties concerned.

"I think you are mad," she stammered.

"I am not mad, and you know I am not mad. Emilia's instinct must have somehow told her this had happened, otherwise she would never have let me come here by myself. She was right. She had nothing to fear. I will go away tomorrow. I can't stay here and see this going on."

"It is all too absurd," said Zita. "I am almost old enough to be his mother."

"As if age had anything to do with those things," said Jean.

Zita knew that however vehemently she might deny and dispute what Jean was saying, she could not find the accents which would make her words sound true. She took refuge in tears, which came all too easily.

Jean melted at the sight.

"My poor child," he said, "it's not your fault that you love him; you can't help it, but I wonder whether he loves you. Not as he ought to in any case; he will make you unhappy. There is nothing to do except for me to go away."

"Don't go away," she said, but there was no real conviction in her voice.

Jean would have given worlds for her to deny the whole thing in accents that he would have believed, but this was just what she did not, what she could not, do.

The band began to play a selection from *Le Petit Duc*.

"I must go and wake Robert," she said, "he told me to wake him directly the band started playing."

Walter Price stayed that night at Nancy, and the next morning Jean left Haréville for the Mont Dore.

# CHAPTER XI

Watering-place life leads to intimacy, and Zita and Walter Price reached, during their stay at Haréville, a pitch of great intimacy, although they were seldom alone together. This did not seem to affect Walter. He was always busy; he always had something to do, and always seemed happy to be a part of the group. He appeared not to want more. Zita did want more, but she could not express her desire, nor do anything to bring it to pass.

As the year before, they took an after-cure at Gérardmer, and then they went home in time for Scotland and the grouse shooting. Robert Harmer invited Price to shoot; he stayed in Scotland a week with them.

After that the lives of the Harmers fell into the old rut; so did Walter's, except that he was sent to Constantinople for several months towards the end of the year. The next year he was in London on and off, but constantly on the move. He managed, nevertheless, to find time to be at Wimbledon. He was getting on in his career, and was often sent on special missions to interview important people or to be on the spot where stirring things were happening. In spite of this, his name had not definitely emerged from the ruck; he was not known outside Fleet Street. Sometimes he would go as far afield as Lisbon or St Petersburg, and sometimes no further than Manchester or Plymouth.

Between these journeys he would find time to go down to

Wimbledon, and so a year passed. The following year the lease on which Harmer had let Wallington came to an end, and he made up his mind to live there again. He let the Wimbledon house, took one in Regent's Park, and settled to spend his holidays at Wallington.

Had anyone told Zita two years previously that when this should happen she would not only not mind it, but positively welcome the change, she would not have believed them. But such was the truth, and the cause of it was that she knew she would see more of Walter. She was blissfully, radiantly happy, and life seemed to begin again for her once more.

When Robert Harmer told Mrs Rylands of the move, she said:

"I am afraid it will be a dreadful blow to Zita to leave that beautiful garden, which is her creation."

"I am afraid it will," said Robert, and he hardly dared broach the topic for a time; but when at last he did so, and stammered something about the garden, all that Zita said was:

"Oh! the garden! We will make one at Wallington. I always thought we could make something wonderful there, but in those days I didn't know enough. I know better now."

Robert Harmer was immensely relieved.

They moved into their London house in the spring and stayed there all the summer. Robert did not go to Harévillethat year. Zita went to Wallington in July. She wished to get everything ready for the autumn. Walter Price happened to be in the neighbourhood 'covering' a by-election, and she saw something of him. Robert had given her carte blanche to do what she liked with the house, and she managed to improve it a little and to make it a little less gloomy and bleak, and she also set about introducing reforms in the garden, and silently undermining the obstinacy of the gardener. Altogether she was ecstatically happy.

They did not go to Scotland that year, but they asked friends for the partridge shooting in September, and a party for the pheasant shooting in November that lasted a week. Mrs Rylands came, and Walter Price was there for a day and a night, which was all he could spare from his work.

Zita stayed at Wallington all the autumn. They paid two visits and came home for Christmas, which the Legges, Mrs Rylands, the Suttons, and Walter Price spent with them.

In January they went to London and stayed there till July, when Robert Harmer, who had not been so well, was told he must do a proper cure at Haréville this year; so they went there in July, accompanied, as usual, by Mrs Rylands, and meeting the Legges there, as usual, again. Walter Price was busy in London, but he hoped, he said, to be able to put in ten days at Haréville; the doctor had told him it would be unwise not to, and like Robert Harmer, he had missed a year and paid for so doing.

They had been a week at Haréville.

Zita was sitting in the park one morning near the band kiosk talking to Amelia Legge.

"I had a letter from Madeleine this morning," said Amelia. "She says that Jean de Bosis is dangerously ill. They are all anxious about him."

"What is it?" said Zita, frightened at her own indifference.

"They don't quite know. He seems to be wasting away – it's a kind of fever."

"Is his wife with him?"

"Oh, yes! Madeleine says she is distracted and nursing him wonderfully. His mother is there too. Poor Jean! They say he worries over his last book, which was not such a success as usual. He has come to think all his books were bad, in spite of his great fame."

"Do you know I have never read one of his books," said Zita, "except that little book of poems, and not all of those."

"It's impossible to get that book now, and not many people have ever heard of it," said Amelia. "I'm sorry he is so unhappy," she added, with a plaintive voice.

"Has he been unhappy?" asked Zita, not looking up.

"Yes, really unhappy. *She* made him unhappy. You see she was too like him, in a way. It was a case of Greek meeting Greek. He ought to have married a quiet, humdrum girl; someone gentle: but the last person he should have chosen was an artist, especially a singer. And Emilia has a terrible temper and Jean is a bundle of nerves. Still, what can one expect? Things so rarely go right. I often think I am not grateful enough having found such a perfect husband as Cyril. When I was younger I used to complain of having to live abroad and go from place to place, but now I know better. I shall never complain. I know how rare perfect husbands are, and I know that I shouldn't have enjoyed a humdrum life in England nearly as much as I've enjoyed our life of travel and bustle and change and interest. I have loved all of it. And you, Zita dear, you ought to be thankful too. You are a happy woman and you have a perfect husband; you couldn't have found a better one. I used to think when you first married that Robert wasn't the right person for you. I know better now. You have a lot to be thankful for."

"Oh, yes," said Zita. "I know I have, and I hope I am grateful."

That morning Zita received a telegram from Walter Price saying he was arriving the same evening. As she read the telegram her heart beat. She had not seen Walter for several months. He had been, on behalf of his newspaper, spending the spring and early summer months in Berlin. He wired from Paris. She would see him that evening. She had never felt so sharp a pang of joy in her life. She was conscious of never having loved him so much. Her whole being seemed to be rushing out towards him. She was ready for anything, any act of sacrifice: she wanted to give everything; to offer – to sacrifice – to surrender.

He arrived before dinner and joined Zita and the Legges.

"You have heard, I suppose," were his first words, "that Jean de Bosis is dead."

They had not heard it.

"Yes; he died early this morning, at four o'clock, of malarial fever, which he caught in Italy. I've got to write his biography, not only for my paper but for America, and I thought you might help me," he said, looking at Zita and Mrs Legge. "I cabled a story this morning. The funeral is to be in the country, and quite quiet – only relations. They are making a big hullabaloo about him in Paris; and the Americans are cabling like hell; his name is popular in the States, he is one of the few European writers that are known there."

"You will be able to help Mr Price," Zita said to Amelia.

"I haven't seen him lately," said Amelia. "I hardly ever saw him after the last time he was here; that was three years ago, when he went away in such a hurry, called to Mont Dore by his wife, who never could leave him out of her sight for five minutes – a genius shouldn't marry a genius. Be careful whom you marry, Mr Price. Don't marry anyone who cares for journalism, or news, or newspapers, or Fleet Street. Find out your opposite."

Walter Price laughed.

"I shall certainly make a wise choice," he said.

Zita quaked inwardly at the thought of his possibly marrying.

"The Americans," said Walter, "want personal stuff about his life. She is well-known in America, too."

"Yes," said Cyril, "they went for a long tour there, she sang, and he gave one or two lectures in English. He told me he hated it, but they made a lot of money, and people were kind to them."

"Yes," said Price, "and they were personally popular. Madame de Bosis has, you see, the international touch; that's what Americans like. They don't like someone who is just all French or just all British – that freezes them."

"Do the Americans like his books?" asked Cyril.

"They have never really read them; but he's a popular personality, on account of his wife. And then some of his books were thought to be scandalous, and they were forbidden in some states, and that all helps from a news point of view."

"Do you think his books will live in France?" asked Cyril.

"Oh, no!" said Walter, "but they are having a good innings and the top of the boom is now, and I am doing my best to boost it more. I'm sorry he's dead, of course, but he has died just at the right moment for me; he couldn't have chosen a better time."

"Poor Jean!" said Amelia.

"He was a white man, and he'll be missed. There was no pretension about him," said Walter.

The next day there were races in the neighbourhood, and Robert Harmer insisted on going. He wanted everyone to go: Mrs Rylands and the Legges consented, but Walter Price did not appear in the morning; he was too busy writing; and Zita said she had a headache. She did not come down in the morning. The others went by train to the races directly after *déjeuner* without her.

After luncheon Zita felt better. She came down and sat in the shade in the park, which was deserted. She sat working, wondering at the fate of Jean de Bosis, and what Walter Price was doing. He answered her question by appearing in person and sitting down next to her.

"I thought you had gone to the races," she said.

"I'm far too busy," he said. "I have roughed out a story, but what I want is the personal touch, and that's just what I can't get."

Zita laughed a little sadly.

"I could supply that," she said, at last.

"You?"

"Yes. I was connected with an odd episode in the life of Jean de Bosis, a long time ago, more than ten years."

"Could I use it? Could it be published?"

"Oh, no."

"Not even in America?"

"Just imagine what Robert would feel!"

"He needn't see it."

"He might, and then…"

"It's a pity, because I suppose it's interesting?"

"It is, or was, interesting to me."

"Is it a love story?"

"Yes."

"Then you had better not tell me. It's too rough. It would have made my whole career."

"Would it?"

"Yes."

"Well, I will tell it you."

"Don't; if you tell it me I shall use it; I shan't be able to flog myself off it."

"Well, you *can* use it; I don't care; I will risk it," she said triumphantly.

The opportunity had come to her at last to make just such a sacrifice as she was longing to make – the supreme sacrifice. Yes, she would face all the consequences, even if it meant leaving Robert. It would prove to Walter how much she loved him.

"I am very fond of you, Walter," she said, almost in a whisper.

"And I am very fond of you," he said, reverently.

"Are you?" she asked, not really understanding the quality of his intonation.

"Yes," he said.

He meant it, but he meant a different fondness from hers. She loved him with passion. He had put her on a pedestal, to worship in a way, but he had never thought of loving her as she dreamt of being loved. She seemed to him quite outside the range of all that.

"Yes," she said, hesitatingly, "I am fond of you. I will prove it you by giving you this story, and you can do what you like with it. After all, you can leave out the names – my name."

And then she began to tell him the story of what had happened long ago in Paris; the story of her early life, of her marriage, her life at Wallington; how she and Robert went to Paris, and how Bertrand had painted her picture, and how she had met Jean de Bosis.

"I was young, and very lovely in those days," she said.

"They say you are still better looking now," said Walter.

Zita knew she was still beautiful, but she knew there was no longer the bloom of youth about her. It had gone for ever. She smiled, and went on.

She told him how she had settled to run away with Jean de Bosis, and how at the last minute she had been unable to.

"I suppose the real reason was I didn't love him. I didn't know then what real love meant; I never knew that till much later."

"And he – was he sore?" asked Walter.

"Yes, he was unhappy and then ill; he nearly died."

"And when did you meet again?"

"Ten years later; the year I first met you here."

"And he loved you still?"

"He said he did."

"And you?"

"It was like a dream to me; I was glad to see him, but I couldn't begin that again, and then…"

"And then what?"

"Well, something happened. I became different; I woke up."

"It's a wonderful story," said Walter. "I can make something big out of it."

"Do you think you can?" she said, feeling an exaltedly secret and fearful joy.

"Sure," he said, "it will make my whole career. There's not a soul who knows it, either?"

"Not a soul. Amelia once had an inkling that something of

the sort might happen, but she never knew."

"I must get busy," said Walter, and he went up to his room, leaving Zita by herself.

She spent the rest of the afternoon alone, till the others came back from the races in time to drink their afternoon glass of water. Zita felt rather like one who has been walking in her sleep and is half aware of having done something tremendous, but does not know what it is.

# CHAPTER XII

At dinner that night Walter Price announced that he would have to leave Haréville the next morning. He had received orders to go to Paris immediately. The Legges were going to the play, as usual, and Harmer and Mrs Ryland spoke of a mild game of *petits chevaux*. Zita said she was tired. And as the party got up to separate, after drinking their coffee on the veranda outside the hotel, Zita said to Walter:

"I shall be in my sitting-room if you have time to come and have a little talk before you go."

"I think I'd better say goodbye now," he said. "I shan't be able to get to bed as it is; I shan't be through with my writing till the morning. I've got the whale of a story on hand," he said, with a glance of gratitude to Zita, "so I'll say goodbye now, Mrs Harmer, and I hope you and Mr Harmer will have a lovely time, and I do thank you from my heart for your great kindness." As he said this he advanced to Mr Harmer, who was just a little bit ahead. Then coming back a step he said, "Goodbye, Mrs Harmer," and he added in a lower tone, "you have done more for me than you know. We shall meet in London in the autumn."

"Yes," said Harmer, "and you must come to Wallington and shoot some partridges."

"Sure," said Price, gaily. "I must say goodbye to Mrs Legge

and Mrs Rylands; I shan't see them in the morning." And he left Zita and Harmer, and caught up Mrs Rylands and the Legges, who had gone on ahead, and said goodbye to them.

Zita went up to her room and waited. She still hoped that Walter Price had spoken as he had done for the benefit of the public, and that he still meant to come and bid her a more private and more intimate goodbye, even if it was only one word. She waited up till eleven, but he never came, and soon after that her husband came in and she went to bed.

She did not see Walter Price again, and when she came down in the morning she was told that he had gone by the earliest train.

The Harmers stayed only another ten days at Haréville, and a week at Gérardmer, and then they went to Wallington.

The day after they arrived, a lovely August day, when the garden was shimmering with heat and there was a pleasant noise of mowing-machines on the lawn, Zita came down early to breakfast, which was at nine, and found awaiting her a letter which she saw at once was in Walter Price's handwriting. She was glad that Robert was not yet down. She opened it. It was a long letter. This is what she read:

*Club, London.*

*Adorable "Queen Guinevere."*

(This name was a joke between them. Walter Price had christened her Queen Guinevere because one day she had said to him: "Robert's name is Arthur as well as Robert, but he can't bear the name, and he can't bear being called Arthur, even in fun," and Walter had said: "That's because he doesn't want you to be Guinevere.")

*I have not had a moment to write since I left Haréville. Things have been humming and a rare lot has happened. I owe all to you. I reckon you know all I have felt for you, although men are pretty dumb when it comes to saying*

91

*anything they mean or feel, but God, fortunately, made
women cute enough to make things square. I'm not
much good at saying things, things that I really feel, but
I suppose you must have some hunch of what I have
always felt for you. I have always, ever since the first
moment I saw you, put you above everyone and
everything else I have known or seen in the world. You
have for me always made the rest of the world look like
thirty cents, as the Americans say. You have been my
good genius, my guardian angel, and have even replaced
in my heart and in my life the place that my sainted
mother once held, and might have held still had she not
been cut away untimely by a cruel disease.*

*You crowned all you did for me by giving me that
story the other day at Haréville. I worked it up, and gave
all my heart to it. Of course I handled the story with the
greatest reverence and reserve, and was careful not only
not to mention your name, but not to say anything
which would betray you to the most cute, nor offend the
most sensitive. I pride myself that it is all in good taste.
Well, the USA Editor – A L Scarp – ate it, and on the
strength of it I have got a permanent post on the
"Illustrated Weekly Moon," the largest illustrated paper
in the States, and the best-selling paper. Thanks to this
I am now able to realize what up to now has been but a
shadowy dream and a teasing mirage. I have for over
two years been engaged secretly to Sylvia Luke, the
daughter of Cuthbert Luke, the great* genre *painter. She
is one in a thousand; a jewel of the first water. I need
not describe her, as you may have seen her pictures in
the shop windows. We have loved each other long, but
marriage seemed up to now an impossible dream. To
make things easier, Sylvia went on the stage and earned
a pittance by playing small parts on tour in vaudeville.
She got some good notices, and folks liked her, but the*

*competition was too great, and her father thought she would do better on the concert stage than on the stage, and lately she has been singing at concerts in the provinces with success – she does imitations. But that is all over now. She need no more work for her living. I have enough for both, and besides a handsome salary, one of the swellest positions in the modern Press. And this is thanks to you, Queen Guinevere – great, generous and noble Fairy Godmother. How we both bless you! Sylvia is longing to know you. I have told her so much about you and talked of you so often that she feels she already knows you intimately. We are to be married at the beginning of September, and in a fortnight's time we sail for the States. We shall live there, but I shall come over to England every summer when things are quiet over there, and I shall not forget the old country, nor Wallington. What more can I say, except that we are grateful to the Fairy Queen who, with a touch of her golden wand, has changed the world for two lovesick mortals? Please give my kindest regards to Mr Harmer.*

Zita read the letter twice. As in a blurred dream, certain odd sights seemed to rise obstinately before her: the first was a small party at Cuthbert Luke's house in St John's Wood. It was an elaborate house – a house furnished as with stage properties. There were a great many palms and brass warming-pans, and some of the rooms were so low you could hardly stand up in them. It was, she remembered, a musical party that night: Robert had refused to go, and she had been by herself. Luke had welcomed the guests in his velvet jacket, and pointed out what he was exhibiting at the Academy – a picture called *After Long Years*, and another called *The Patrician's Daughter*. The painter's technique was admirable.

A pianist had played Hungarian dances; a violinist had played *Simple Aveu*; a tenor had sung 'I'll sing thee songs of

Araby'; and 'Maid of Athens', and, finally, the daughter of the house had stepped on to the platform. There was no pressing, because she regarded herself as a professional. She was overwhelmingly blond – what would now be called a 'platinum blonde', but the word had not then been invented. She had light grey eyes and a dazzling row of teeth. She did a few imitations – some with music, some without – of Letty Lind, Florence St John, Marie Lloyd, Violet Cameron, Arthur Roberts, and Ellen Terry. She caught and reproduced the accent of the stage and the mannerism of the originals exactly, but there was not a spark of fancy or of humour in her impersonations.

And then Zita remembered walking down the Burlington Arcade one day and seeing in a shop window a photograph of the same dazzling blonde with flashing teeth, and under it was printed: 'Miss Sylvia Luke'. This was rare in those days, unless the sitter was an actress or a singer of note, and Sylvia Luke as an artiste was unknown to the public; but she was known as a beauty, well-known enough to have her name printed on the photographs that were for sale in the Burlington Arcade.

The third snapshot that floated across Zita's memory was one day at Brighton; she was shopping, and looking at the window of a second-hand jeweller's shop full of pretty silver and quaint ornaments, when she caught sight of Sylvia Luke and her father, who were looking at the same shop window.

She only heard Sylvia say two words before she and her father walked on. They were:

"They're false." And in these two words she managed to instil the maximum of contempt with the minimum of refinement.

Then one day, when Wilfrid Sutton was having tea with her, and the subject of Cuthbert Luke's pictures happened to crop up, Zita asked Wilfrid whether he knew Sylvia Luke, as he knew most people in the theatrical and Bohemian world.

"Oh, yes," he said, "she's a good girl. Good-hearted and respectable; no use on the stage. She can't act for nuts, and she can't sing. She has a gift of mimicry, and she can reproduce the sound of some people's voices exactly, but she isn't funny, and she has no sense of humour, so she can't make it amusing,and it ends by being rather a bore; but she's good-looking and a good sort, and she's greatly admired and liked. Lots of people have wanted to marry her."

That conversation had taken place a year ago, and now...

She walked to the sideboard and she noticed that in Robert's place there was a large roll that might contain an illustrated newspaper.

'Perhaps,' she thought, 'that contains Sylvia Luke's picture.' And she helped herself to eggs and bacon. Robert was late; so late that she rang the bell and asked whether he was not yet up.

The butler said that he had had breakfast early, and had gone out riding; he would be back presently. Zita finished breakfast; looked at a newspaper; saw the cook; ordered dinner, that is to say, checked the bill of fare that had already been glanced at by Robert; answered some letters and walked into the garden as far as the gardener's house, which was at the end of the kitchen-garden. She wanted to see the gardener. She found him and discussed one or two matters, cut some flowers for the house, and then strolled back to the house.

'What a lovely day,' she said to herself, 'even Wallington is beautiful today.'

When she got back to the house she was met by Clark, the butler, who had been with them ever since they were married. Mr Harmer had been obliged to go suddenly to London, he said. He had gone by the ten forty-five. He wanted her to follow by the five o'clock train. He had ordered the carriage, and her things were being packed. The caretaker had been informed by telegraph.

"Did he tell the kitchen-maid to go?" Zita asked.

"Yes, madam. He said that she was to go tomorrow."

"Didn't he leave a letter or a message for me?"

Clarke shook his head, and said "No" – sadly, thought Zita. A curious feeling as of a nightmare began to creep over her.

"Mr Harmer said he would explain everything in London; he had only just time to catch the train, and as it was he nearly missed it, so Charles (the coachman) said."

"Oh, that accounts for everything," said Zita; but she thought it accounted for nothing.

Before luncheon the second post arrived, and with it a large illustrated newspaper in a roll for her. 'That's just like the one which came for Robert this morning,' Zita thought. She opened it, and her eye fell at once on an article called 'The Life Romance of Jean de Bosis.' There was the story, exactly as she had told it to Walter, with every particle of emphasis, accentuation and vulgarity that headlines, captions, and all the artifices of publicity, as far as they went at that epoch, could give. The captions were terrible: 'Lovely bride homesick in Parisian home': 'Thwarted poet meets his soul-mate': 'Famous painter throws starving souls together': 'Scared wife jibs at the last fence'.

Zita read through the article from beginning to end. The whole story was there. Her name was not mentioned, but short of that everything was said, and her picture by Bertrand was produced as an example of his art – as though by accident. There was the story of her life, trumpeted to the world on the loudest of brass instruments, and blazoned in letters of limelight.

'Well, had she not foreseen this might, this *must* happen?' Not quite like that; and then at that moment she had been prepared not to mind because she thought that Walter loved her, or might love her, but now…

'Robert has seen this,' she said to herself; 'he will turn me out of the house.'

She went into his study. In the fireplace there was a litter of envelopes which had been thrown away, and among other

96

rubbish she saw the charred remains of the wrapper that had held the *Illustrated Weekly Moon.*

Zita found that her maid had received instructions to pack and go to London with her. She arrived in London at seven o'clock and found the caretaker waiting for her.

Mr Harmer, she said, was staying at the club; but dinner was ready. The caretaker had cooked a chicken and rice pudding. There was also a letter awaiting her that had been sent by hand. It was from the family solicitor, Mr Hanson, saying Mr Harmer wished him to see her the next morning at his office, and would she kindly call at Lincoln's Inn at eleven o'clock.

Zita arrived punctually at Mr Hanson's office at eleven o'clock the next morning. Mr Hanson received her like a father and plunged gently into the matter, talking in a soothing diminuendo. He did not refer to the cause or the reason, the why or the wherefore; he just stated the fact that Mr Harmer had suggested a separation by mutual consent, and was willing to make his wife an adequate allowance. Mr Harmer had no wish to divorce, and he supposed she would not wish it either. Would she be willing to agree to this arrangement? Oral consent was sufficient, but it was more usual to draw up a deed, and that was the course Mr Harmer preferred. If she was willing, all that she would have to do would be to sign the deed when it was drawn up. There were certain minor questions of detail as to chattels to settle.

Zita said at once she was more than willing. Mr Hanson gave a sigh of relief. Mr Harmer was anxious for her to live in the London house until she should find a house that suited her. He had even arranged for a kitchen-maid to come up to London from Wallington to cook for her and to stay as long as should be necessary. He himself would be returning to Wallington as soon as the deed was signed.

"You understand," said Mr Hanson, "the separation will be immediate."

Zita said she quite understood. A further appointment was made for the signing of the deed, and the interview came to an end. Zita was determined to find a house as soon as possible. She found one the next day in Dulwich Village: a furnished cottage with a small garden, and in a fortnight's time she had moved in. Robert Harmer had told her, through Mr Hanson, that he would send her all her personal effects, but she refused to keep any of the jewels or anything that he had given her, and she had few things of her own.

She never saw Robert again. He died two years later during an epidemic of influenza. Before he died he had sold both his London house and his house at Wimbledon. He left Zita the same allowance she had received during his lifetime. He left a legacy to Amelia Legge, and Wallington went to the next of kin, a nephew who had settled in Canada, and who died five years later, leaving a son. This boy, Kenneth Harmer, became a cadet in the navy, and was a midshipman in 1914. He did well in the war and after. He used to go and see Zita when he was on leave, and she must have liked him, as she left him the small patrimony she had inherited from her mother, and the works of Tennyson.

Zita Harmer lived at Dulwich for the rest of her life, and died at the age of seventy, in 1920. She made her little garden beautiful, but she seldom saw anyone, and she never met Walter Price again. He settled down in America for good. The Legges used to visit her when they were in England. Legge died, an ambassador, a few years before the war: Amelia lived till the end of the war, but mostly abroad. She died the same year as Mrs Harmer.

Zita was a beautiful old lady. Her hair was white and there were many tiny wrinkles on her lovely skin; but in her carriage, her movements, and her walk were the authority that only great beauty and the certainty of having possessed it confer, and her smile still lit up a whole room. People who would see her walking in Dulwich Village and Dulwich Park would wonder who she was, and what her story had been – that is to say, if she had had a story, which they thought unlikely.

They called her the 'Lonely Lady'.

# CHAPTER XIII

I was at Dulwich when the effects of Mrs Harmer were being sold by auction in her cottage. The effects were mostly ordinary Victorian furniture, which was of no interest or importance, and went for little. There were a great many books, but with the exception of an odd collection of novels, they were mostly about gardening and technical at that. Mrs Harmer must have been a serious gardener.

There were no pictures in the house except one or two early Victorian engravings by Landseer and Frith, which she had found there when she had taken the house. She had changed nothing in the furniture or the decoration, and had introduced no furniture of her own.

There was an early Broadwood pianoforte, which made a wheezy tinkling noise like a spinet. I should have liked to buy that, had I known what to do with it. I went all over the little house before the sale, and visited the garden. It was a small garden, but it had been evidently planted and tended by a master hand and a loving mind.

The sale took place towards the end of June, and the Madonna lilies were out; and the garden was curiously aromatic with verbena and sweet-scented geranium, cherry-pie and stocks, and sweet william and pinks. The cottage walls were smothered in roses. It was an unpretentious garden, and yet there was something special about it; something rare and intensely individual. This was odd, because in the house there was nothing that gave one the slightest indication of anything individual or personal. Inthe bedroom there was a cheap crucifix and a large coloured lithograph of the Holy Family.

I bought two lots at the sale: a French book and an old-fashioned leather workbox or writing-desk – I don't know which, for it contained reels of silk, tapestry needles, a crochet hook and a half-finished kettle-holder with 'A Merry Christmas' begun but not finished on it, as well as pens, pencils, an inkpot and a little notebook, and some sealing-wax and a seal.

The French book was an old one, published in eighteen-eighty. It was tattered, but only half cut; it was a little bookof verse called *Stances*. On the title-page there was an inscription in violet ink: 'à Madame Harmer, avec les plus respectueux hommages de Jean de Bosis, Paris, le 3 Mai, 1880'. One day I was looking at the writing-desk or workbox, and I took out the little notebook. I found it contained three entries in pencil. One was headed:

'New Year's Day, 1894.
"So far, that my doom is, I love thee still.
Let no man dream but that I love thee still."

Underneath this was written 'Guinevere'.

Further on in the book was another entry:

'Good Friday, 1900.
"Amor meus Crucifixus est."

There was a third entry, dated 'May, 1920'. It must have been written just before she died. It was to this effect: 'Kenneth came to tea'.

'Secure for a full due.'

I took out the small gold seal from the box, but I could not distinguish the image nor decipher the superscription. Out of curiosity, I took an impression. The image was that of a face enclosed in a heart, from which a flame arose, and the inscription was:

*Saignant et brûlant.*

# MAURICE BARING

## 'C'

Baring's homage to a decadent and carefree Edwardian age depicts a society as yet untainted by the traumas and complexities of twentieth-century living. With wit and subtlety, a happy picture is drawn of family life, house parties in the country and a leisured existence clouded only by the rumblings of the Boer War. Against this spectacle Caryl Bramsley (the 'C' of the title) is presented – a young man of terrific promise but scant achievement, whose tragicomic tale offsets the privileged milieu.

## CAT'S CRADLE

This sophisticated and intricate novel, based on true events, takes place in the late nineteenth century and begins with Henry Clifford, a man of taste and worldly philosophy, whose simple determination to do as he likes and live as he wishes is threatened when his daughter falls in love with an unsuitable man. With subtle twists and turns in a fascinating portrait of society, Maurice Baring conveys the moral that love is too strong to be overcome by mere mortals.

# MAURICE BARING

## THE COAT WITHOUT SEAM

The story of a miraculous relic, believed to be a piece of the seamless coat worn by a soldier on Mount Golgotha after Jesus of Nazareth's crucifixion, captivates young Christopher Trevenen after his sister dies tragically and motivates the very core of his existence from then on, culminating in a profound and tragic realization.

## DAPHNE ADEANE

Barrister Basil Wake and his arresting wife Hyacinth lead a well-appointed existence in the social whirl of London's early 1900s. For eight years Hyacinth has conducted a most discreet affair with Parliamentarian Michael Choyce, who seems to fit into the Wakes' lives so conveniently. But an invitation to attend a Private View and a startling portrait of the mysterious and beautiful Daphne Adeane signifies a change in this comfortable set-up.

# Maurice Baring

## In My End Is My Beginning

This historical novel tells the tragic story of Mary Queen of Scots, from her childhood until the beginning of her end, whose unwise marital and political actions provoked rebellion among Scottish nobles and forced her to flee to England, where she was beheaded as a Roman Catholic threat to the throne. The clash of opinion over whether Mary was a martyr or a murderess is perfectly represented by four eye-witnesses(The Four Maries – her ladies-in-waiting) who narrate this captivating story with distinctive conclusions.

## Tinker's Leave

Reserved and unworldly, young Miles Consterdine and his epiphanic trip to Paris is Maurice Baring's first bead on this thread of a story based on impressions received by the author in Russia and Manchuria during wartime. From here Baring allows us to peek through windows opening onto tragic and comic episodes in the lives of noteworthy people in remarkable circumstances.